Acclaim for **Ralph Ellison**'s

FLYING HOME
and Other Stories

"Eye-opening . . . remarkable. . . . Ellison puts to shame most of this season's new story collections. . . . Anyone who thinks writers are made, not born, should read *Flying Home.*"
—*New York Observer*

"We witness Ellison's increasingly assured control of language, his experiments with black folklore and his refining of his great themes. . . . Reading *Flying Home* . . . is much like listening to some young musician riffing on the changes of older, more experienced artists until, eventually and inevitably, he slips the breaks and finds his own voice, soaring on wings of song."
—*Washington Post*

"Ripe with the forceful musicality, unmistakable politics, and fine promise of one of our best-ever black writers."
—*Elle*

"Marvelous. . . . Glorious, pre–*Invisible Man* riffs—and another fine addition to the Ellison oeuvre."
—*Kirkus Reviews*

About the Author

Ralph Ellison was born in Oklahoma City in 1914. He is the author of *Invisible Man* (1952), which won the National Book Award and became one of the most important and influential postwar American novels. He published two volumes of nonfiction, *Shadow and Act* (1964) and *Going to the Territory* (1986), which, together with unpublished speeches and writings, were brought together as *The Collected Essays of Ralph Ellison* in 1995. For more than forty years before his death in 1994, Ralph Ellison lived with his wife, Fanny McConnell, on Riverside Drive in Harlem in New York City.

About the Editor

John F. Callahan was born in Meriden, Connecticut. He is Morgan S. Odell Professor of Humanities at Lewis and Clark College in Portland, Oregon. His books include *The Illusions of a Nation* and *In the African-American Grain.* He is the editor of the Modern Library edition of *The Collected Essays of Ralph Ellison* and is literary executor of Ralph Ellison's estate.

Also by **Ralph Ellison**

Invisible Man

Shadow and Act

Going to the Territory

The Collected Essays of Ralph Ellison

FLYING HOME
and Other Stories

Fiction

Ralph Ellison
25 Hamilton Tr.
NYC

I DID NOT LEARN THEIR NAMES

It was chilly up on top. We were riding up to St. Louis on a manifest, clinging to the top of a boxcar. It was dark and sparks from the engine flew back to where we were riding. Sometimes cinders flew in our faces and the thick, tumbling part of the blackness was smoke. The freight jerked and bumped and the sparks flew past, dancing red in the whirling blackness. It was chilly as hell and we were traveling fast. The Santa Fe freight was high-balling down a grade in the dark. Miles off to our left an airport beacon carved the night. (It was cold up on top for early fall and) The cinders struck our faces like sand whirled in the wind.

" How soon'll we make it to St. Louis?" I yelled to Morrie.

" Tommorrow noon, if she dont jump the track. She's running like a bitch with the itch," he yelled in my ear.

Morrie was my buddy. I had met him in the sunflower jungle outside an Oklahoma town. He climbed off when the freight stopped and sat near me on the embankment. It had given me a queer feeling as I watched him roll up his trousers and take off his leg. The artificial leg had been flesh-white and the stump red and raw. . He had lost his leg to the knee beneath the wheels of a freight and the artificial leg had been given him by an insurance company. He told me he had been on the bum for five years. The next day he had saved me from falling between two cars to the wheels below and he recieved quiet a kick from having a Negro for a buddy.

An old couple was riding in the car below us. I had seen them climb quietly into the boxcar when the freight had made its last stop at dusk.

Ralph Ellison

FLYING HOME

and Other Stories

Edited and with an Introduction by
John F. Callahan

VINTAGE INTERNATIONAL
Vintage Books
A Division of Random House, Inc.
New York

FIRST VINTAGE INTERNATIONAL EDITION, JANUARY 1998

 Published in the United States by Vintage Books, a division of Random House, Inc., New York, and simultaneously in Canada by Random House of Canada Limited, Toronto. Originally published in hardcover in the United States by Random House, Inc., New York, in 1996.

Editor's Note:
The version of "Hymie's Bull" published herein has been edited from both Ellison's manuscripts and the galleys from *New Challenge,* where it was originally scheduled for publication in 1937; hence the differences between the story here and the version in the Random House hardcover first edition of *Flying Home and Other Stories*.

Reproduction of a typescript page on page 175 from Ralph Ellison's unpublished, untitled reminiscence on becoming a writer. Reproduced from the Collections of the Library of Congress. Photos on pages iv and 175 courtesy of Fanny Ellison.

Library of Congress Cataloging-in-Publication Data
Ellison, Ralph.
Flying home and other stories / Ralph Ellison : edited and with an introduction by John F. Callahan.—1st Vintage International ed.
p. cm.
ISBN 0-679-77661-3 (pbk.)
1. Afro-Americans—Social life and customs—Fiction.
I. Callahan, John F., 1940- . II. Title.
PS3555.L625F58 1997
813'.54—dc21 97-12393
CIP

Random House Web address: http://www.randomhouse.com

Printed in the United States of America
10 9 8

Contents

Introduction by John F. Callahan ix

A Party Down at the Square 3

Boy on a Train 12

Mister Toussan 22

Afternoon 33

That I Had the Wings 45

A Coupla Scalped Indians 63

Hymie's Bull 82

I Did Not Learn Their Names 89

A Hard Time Keeping Up 97

The Black Ball 110

King of the Bingo Game 123

In a Strange Country 137

Flying Home 147

Introduction

1.

"You could never tell where you were going," Ralph Ellison's Invisible Man observed, musing over the twists and turns of his fate. "You started looking for red men and you found them—even though of a different tribe and in a bright new world." So it was with Ellison's discovery of his identity as a writer. And so it is with this collection of his short fiction.

"I blundered into writing," Ellison admitted in a 1961 interview with novelist Richard G. Stern. At first, in Oklahoma from the time he was eight and his mother bought him a used cornet, music was his life. As a high school student, Ellison cut the grass in exchange for trumpet lessons from the conductor Ludwig Hebestreit, who, impressed with his earnestness and talent, also gave him impromptu instruction in orchestration. In 1933, according to his unpublished "Autobiographical Notes," written before the publication of *Invisible Man,* after "operating an elevator two years at eight dollars a week in a vain effort to save tuition fees," he was awarded a scholarship to Tuskegee Institute to study symphonic composition and trumpet with the famed William L. Dawson, whose Tuskegee choir opened Radio City. Unable to afford train fare, he made his way from Oklahoma City to Alabama, hoboing on the freights of half a dozen railroads.

A year after coming to New York in the summer of 1936, hoping—vainly it turned out—to earn the money for his senior-year tuition, Ellison met and struck up a friendship with Richard Wright. Having finished but not yet found a publisher for his first book, *Uncle Tom's Children,* Wright encouraged Ellison to review a novel for the fall 1937 issue of *New Challenge,* which he co-edited. Ellison complied. "My review was accepted and published," he recalled, "and so I was hooked." Yet one review does not make a writer, let alone turn a musician into a fiction writer. Once again Wright intervened, and the shadow of Ellison's destiny moved closer to the act. "On the basis of this review," Ellison recalled, "Wright suggested that I try a short story, which I did," again for *New Challenge.* "I tried to use my knowledge of riding freight trains. He liked the story well enough to accept it, and it got as far as the galley proofs, when it was bumped from the issue because there was too much material. Just after that the magazine failed." The story was "Hymie's Bull," and at the top of the first page of the final typescript, Ellison drew a rectangle around the year 1937 in emphatic black ink. Just where he wrote his apparent first story is not clear. Perhaps he began it in New York, where, after a fling at sculpture, he was still trying to be a musician. Life in New York that summer of 1937 was chaotic for Ellison. Like many with artistic aspirations who came of age in the 1930s, Ellison also agitated on behalf of

Republican Spain, and was involved in the campaign for the release of the Scottsboro boys, nine young black men convicted and sentenced to death on trumped-up charges of gang-raping two white women in a boxcar in Alabama.

Meanwhile, in Dayton, Ohio, Ellison's mother, Mrs. Ida Bell, who had moved there from Oklahoma City the year before, fell from a porch, and her actual condition—tuberculosis of the hip—was gravely misdiagnosed as arthritis. In mid-October Ellison arrived in Ohio. With only a single short story in progress to his credit, he had no idea he was at the edge of a drastic change in his life. He expected to stay only long enough to see his mother through her illness and convalescence. But he was wrong. And his experience wrenched him away from the inner moorings he thought he had made fast the previous four years at Tuskegee and in New York.

In a letter headed "Dear Folks," dated October 17, 1937, written from Dayton, probably to relatives or friends back in Oklahoma City, he tells what he had found a few days earlier at the Cincinnati hospital to which his mother had gone when her condition suddenly worsened. "I arrived in Cinn. on Friday at 5:45 to find my mother leaving, and she in such a condition that she was unable to recognize me. At 11:00 next day she was gone. She was in such pain that she knew no one. It is the worse [sic] thing that has ever happened and I can't explain the emptiness." Ten days later he writes Richard Wright that his mother's death marked the end of his childhood. Unlike the pretense of change he'd felt on coming to New York, the loss of his mother "is real, and the most final thing I've ever encountered." His mother's illness and unexpected death became a painful catalyst, for, as Ellison later told it in *Shadow and Act,* it was "during the period I started trying seriously to write and that was the breaking point."

"You have to leave home to find home," Ellison, years later, scribbled in the margin of a page of his novel in progress. And that October 1937, stranded in Dayton and emptied of emotion, Ellison, like his future character Invisible Man, descended into the abyss of himself, confronted the darkness, and emerged resolved to write his way through the pain and loss. If "geography was fate," as Ellison liked to say of his Oklahoma birth and upbringing, in Dayton fate followed from geography. Before long, an ambassador from the gods appeared in the form of Lawyer Stokes. One of the first black attorneys in Dayton and a man whose youngest son was Ellison's age, William O. Stokes befriended the motherless, fatherless stranger. Seeing Ellison take refuge in a nearby restaurant and scrawl away in a cheap spiral notebook, Lawyer Stokes gave the young man a key to his law office. Consequently, as Ellison told it in a 1985 letter to his old friend Mamie Rhone, "some of my earliest efforts at writing fiction were done on his typewriter and stationery." (In fact, manuscripts of several early unpublished stories were typed on letterhead of the Montgomery County Republican Executive Committee, Colored Section, an organization that had four committeemen, one of whom was Atty. W. O. Stokes.)

Stokes was Ellison's benefactor in more fundamental ways. "When my brother Herbert and I had lost our living quarters, Lawyer Stokes allowed us to sleep in his office and make use of its toilet and bathing facilities." A staunch Lincoln Republican despite the Depression and the emergence of Franklin D. Roosevelt, Stokes argued politics with Ellison, then a self-described young radical, who wrote on October 27, 1937, from what he called his "exile" in Dayton, to Richard Wright in New York, that "there is no *Daily [Worker]* nor *[New] Masses* to be had here"; and on November 8, "all I have here is the *New Republic* and the radio." Ellison recalled this "most incongruous and instructive friendship" with Lawyer Stokes in his 1985 letter to Mamie Rhone, confessing that Stokes's "aid and encouragement" had helped him through "what seemed a period of hopelessness."

Stokes's friendship and hospitality to Ellison, after the desolation caused by his mother's passing, must have conjured up memories of Mr. J. D. (for Jefferson Davis) Randolph, custodian of the State Law Library back in Oklahoma City and self-taught expert in the law, who had treated Ralph like a kinsman in the wake of his father Lewis's death. Having once more lost closest kin, the young Ellison again found kith, this time in Lawyer Stokes. In effect, Stokes showed him the way home. He gave him shelter in his office, engaged his mind, and, by encouraging him to know his work as a writer, helped him prepare to emerge as a man in the world. Little wonder Ellison told Wright that he found the streets of Dayton "very much like those of Oklahoma City, home." In Dayton he was not as lucky finding odd jobs as he had been while growing up in Oklahoma City. He lived hand to mouth and, as he told Wright, spent most of his time in the woods picking "pears growing wild" and gathering walnuts and "fine full flavored butter nuts." In the cold, snowy surrounding countryside, relying on Ernest Hemingway's prose and what he'd learned shooting game with his stepfather in the Oklahoma brush, he hunted rabbit, quail, and pheasant for his living. In his essay "February," written almost twenty years later, Ellison remembers his discovery of a single apple on the ground, "preserved by the leaves and grasses, protected by the snows." He remembers the serene, poignant beauty of a cock quail dead by his gun, and he remembers his sudden exhilaration at having come through the barren fields of his mother's death and "crossed over into a new phase of living." Like the subsequent journey of fellow Tuskegeean Albert Murray in *South to a Very Old Place,* Ellison traveled from New York City west to a very old place, and found Oklahoma in Ohio.

Ellison closed his November 8 letter to Richard Wright with the words "Workers of the World Must Write!!!!" He wasn't kidding. And what he did not say—but what manuscripts of his early unpublished stories make clear—is that, after hours, in Lawyer Stokes's office, Ralph Ellison became a writer. In Dayton during the seven months from October 1937 to April 1938, he wrote drafts or partial drafts of several stories, two or three sketches, and more than a hundred pages of a novel referred to simply as *Slick*—a work he abandoned but which survives as a substantial fragment. In this new world, memories of his former life in Oklahoma fought through layers of loss and grief, and Ellison used the hurt as a passport to literature's country of the imagination.

2.

Like Odysseus, Ellison faced what in his essay "Tell It Like It Is, Baby" he was to call "our orphan's loneliness." Seeking the way home, he came to realize that home's true geography lay within. New York was the future he aimed at, Oklahoma the country of memory, and Dayton the strangely familiar spot of his life's crossroads. Years later, in the Introduction to *Shadow and Act,* he told how in his most secret heart he continued to regard himself as a musician. But during those seven months in Dayton he untied the Gordian knot of his "complicated, semiconscious strategy of self-deception, a refusal by my right hand [the musician's] to recognize where my left hand [the writer's] was headed." Musician and writer remained enough in cahoots for Ellison's artistic identity to emerge in an ambidextrous, advantageous equilibrium between music and literature. The young man who had dreamed of composing a symphony by the time he turned twenty-six pledged allegiance to the novelists' tribe and ended up writing *Invisible Man,* a novel with traces of symphonic form as well as the beat and breaks of jazz.

Though a first novel, *Invisible Man* was an artistic culmination, for in Dayton, and for a good while afterward in New York, Ellison was an apprentice slowly mastering his craft. Earlier, he had learned his lesson the hard way as an aspiring musician at Tuskegee. In "The Little Man at Chehaw Station" (a whistle-stop not far from Tuskegee) he remembered a public recital wherein, "substituting a certain skill of lips and fingers for the intelligent and artistic structuring of emotion," he suffered embarrassing, withering criticism from his teachers. More soothing and salutary was the scolding administered in private by Hazel Harrison, the concert pianist and confidante who, while in Europe, had enjoyed the respect of Ferruccio Busoni and Sergei

Prokofiev. Harrison's honesty gave Ellison the key to the relationship between the artist and his audience—"you must *always* play your best, even if it's only in the waiting room at Chehaw Station, because in this country there'll always be a little man hidden behind the stove" and "he'll know the *music,* and the *tradition,* and the standards of *musicianship* required for whatever you set out to perform." Harrison's words made a deep impression on Ellison. Embracing a very stern discipline, he resolved to perform or write always as if the little man at Chehaw Station were looking over his shoulder.

In an undated meditation, Ellison traces his commitment to that same "structuring of emotion" he had once neglected as a trumpet player at Tuskegee. He recapitulates the impact of three nineteenth-century novels—*Wuthering Heights, Jude the Obscure, Crime and Punishment*—when, as an undergraduate, he first discovered the artistic power of fiction. "Oddly enough," he adds, as if already possessed of the writer's soul, "these works which so moved me did not move me to the extent of trying to write fiction." Instead, it took a poem, T. S. Eliot's *The Waste Land,* which Ellison discovered at Tuskegee in 1935, to stimulate the wild idea that fiction, not music, might be his true art form. Ever loyal to his musician's bent, while his eye read Eliot's fragments, his ear heard Louis Armstrong's "two hundred choruses on the theme of 'Chinatown.' " And it was mastery of tradition, vernacular and classical, Ellison felt, that enabled jazzman and poet alike, in Invisible Man's words, to "slip into the breaks and look around," then improvise in an original individual style.

Ellison's reminiscence does not solve the mystery of why

an aspiring symphonic composer and trumpet player would be moved toward fiction from creative expression in music. But moved he was, though moved in the still waters below the surface of his conscious ambition to compose symphonies. Ellison followed up on *The Waste Land* by reading Edmund Wilson's 1931 study of the moderns, *Axel's Castle,* with its concluding stiff drink of Soviet Marxism, then the sources mentioned in Eliot's notes and as many other modern poets and their critics as he could get his hands on. There were plenty in Tuskegee's library, and it was a lifelong source of pride and gladness for Ellison to have discovered Eliot and Joyce, Pound and Yeats, Conrad, Stein, Hemingway, and others at his school, and read them first there.

Finally, in the same account of his first stirrings as a writer, Ellison remembers the epiphany of Hemingway's prose—how "its spell became like a special iris to my eyes through which scenes and physical action took on a new vividness." Later, writing stories like "Flying Home," and still later, in *Invisible Man,* Ellison finds the American language and his African-American tradition more expansive, fluid, and eclectic than the hard-boiled utterance and attitude often favored by Hemingway. But as a young man trying to learn to write during the thirties, "in the work of Hemingway I discovered something of that same teasing quality that had moved me in the poetry, that quality of implying much more than was stated explicitly." This technique, Ellison recognized, presented certain difficulties, difficulties that were next of kin to the challenges of his peculiar American condition. "For I found," he observed in the Introduction to *Shadow and Act,* that "the greatest difficulty for a Negro writer was the problem of revealing what he truly felt, rather than serving up what Negroes were supposed to feel, and were encouraged to feel."

Learning to write, Ellison amends Hemingway's creed. He does not seize upon Hemingway's difficulty of "knowing truly what you really felt"; rather, conscious of the dangers implicit (and explicit) in being a member of the Negro minority in the United States, he stresses not the question of knowing what he felt—he knew that—but the rhetorical problem of how to express it. (This will be Ellison's genius in *Invisible Man:* From the opening assertion—"I am an invisible man"—to his closing question—"Who knows but that, on the lower frequencies, I speak for you?"—the eponymous protagonist narrates *how* he feels in a progression of jazz breaks taking off from and returning to the bass line of invisibility.) Was Ellison thinking of the breaks, the syncopations, the swing of jazz when he wrote in that same reflection on becoming a writer that Hemingway's prose "did not move straightforwardly as did the familiar prose I knew, and its rhythms were shorter and circular"?

Ellison notes that Hemingway "could distill the great emotion from the most deadpan, casual-appearing, understated effects." Hemingway's courage in taking on the "difficulties of convention" and the rhythms and "understated effects of his prose" appealed to Ellison's sense of his own artistic situation. So it was, he explains, that "several years later when I started trying to write fiction, I selected Hemingway for a model." As a college student, he had read Hemingway's stories in barbershop copies of *Esquire* and his books in the Tuskegee library. Later, in the winter of 1937–38, when he began to feel the writer's fever, Ellison recalled in a 1984 letter to John Roche, he "walked a mile or so from the Negro section into downtown Dayton" every day to find a copy of *The New York Times* and "read Hemingway's dispatches from the Spanish Civil War which [he] studied for style as well as information."

For young Ellison style was the donnée of art and personality. As a boy living in a state changing rapidly from a frontier territory to the Oklahoma of both the infamous Tulsa riot of 1921 and the hokum and Jim Crow spawned by perennial candidate and eventual governor "Alfalfa Bill" Murray, Ellison yearned, he wrote later in *Shadow and Act,* "to make any-and-everything of quality Negro American—to appropriate it, possess it, re-create it in our own group and individual images." Along with several African-American Oklahoma boyhood friends, he dreamed of becoming a Renaissance man in no small part because of the elegant assertions of style by men most would never have associated with such an exalted idea. "Gamblers and scholars, jazz musicians and scientists, Negro cowboys and soldiers from the Spanish-American and First World wars, movie stars and stunt men, figures from the Italian Renaissance and literature, both classical and popular, were combined with the special virtues of some local bootlegger, the eloquence of some Negro preacher, the strength and grace of some local athlete, the ruthlessness of some businessman-physician, the elegance in dress and manners of some headwaiter or hotel doorman." From these individuals Ellison and his friends sought to create composite models of self. Although these types do not show up per se in his early fiction, the style and feel of their attempts to subvert the world and make reality over in their image mark Ellison's prose.

3.

After *Invisible Man,* Ellison's fiction was given over almost entirely to his novel in progress. And this project, after the amazing, unanticipated success of his first novel, accentuated his natural penchant to revise, revise, revise, and only slowly come to satisfaction about his work. Nonetheless, more than once during the last year of his life, the short stories came to the forefront of Ellison's consciousness.

The last time I saw him in his apartment before his final illness—on a cold, bright February afternoon ten days shy of his eightieth birthday, in 1994—Ellison spoke of the novel—"the damn transitions are still giving me fits, but I'm having fun"—and then he told me that he wanted to publish his short stories. (A few months earlier, I had collected the published stories and sent them to him in a loose-leaf binder.) Now he hinted that there might be more, and joked about the files crammed into what Mrs. Ellison called "the little room," off the long, book-teeming hallway of their apartment. But soon he turned his attention to the window and a lone seagull breasting the whitecaps that blew across the Hudson River below. And I forgot his words about the stories until another windy afternoon two Februaries later when I was hunting for a certain section of the novel.

"John," Mrs. Ellison said. "There's a box under the dining room table. Have a look." I rummaged through it, and at the bottom, beneath old magazines, clippings, and duplicate printouts from the novel, I discovered a brown imitation-leather folder with RALPH W. ELLISON embossed in gold letters on the front. Inside, bulging with manuscripts, was a manila folder labeled "Early Stories." The stories were typed on paper brown with age and beginning to crumble;

here and there passages were crossed out, and revisions inserted in Ralph's hand.

I realized these were stories that had never been published, never been mentioned—stories no one knew about. To my surprise I found that even Mrs. Ellison didn't know about them, and subsequently, with one or two exceptions, I have not come across mention of the stories in Ellison's papers. In any case this cache of stories gave impetus and shape to the present collection. Initially, I had put off collecting Ellison's previously published stories because eight of the pieces—"And Hickman Arrives" (1960); "The Roof, the Steeple and the People" (1960); "It Always Breaks Out" (1963); "Juneteenth" (1965); "Night-Talk" (1969); "A Song of Innocence" (1970); "Cadillac Flambé" (1973), and "Backwacking: A Plea to the Senator" (1977)—were selections from the novel in progress, stories whose fate should await publication of the novel. "Did You Ever Dream Lucky?" (1954) and "Out of the Hospital and Under the Bar" (1963), told by or about Ellison's indispensable folk character Mary Rambo, were offshoots or originally part of *Invisible Man.* "Slick Gonna Learn" (1939) and, perhaps indirectly, "The Birthmark" (1940) were related to the *Slick* novel begun in Dayton and then abandoned for good not long afterward.

Discovery of the more than half-dozen early stories made it possible to put together a volume of Ellison's best published and unpublished freestanding fiction. From the former I have included the three early Buster-and-Riley stories "Mister Toussan" (1941), "Afternoon" (1940), and "That I Had the Wings" (1943), and latter-day brother to these, "A Coupla Scalped Indians" (1956). (In a batch of notes from

1954 or 1955, Ellison referred to "A Coupla Scalped Indians" as a Buster-and-Riley story, but before publication in 1956, he dropped Riley in favor of an unnamed narrator, perhaps because he thought he might blend the story into the Oklahoma chapters projected for his recently begun second novel. But in the end he did not, and so the story stands as a coda to the earlier Buster-and-Riley fictions.) Three other stories, "In a Strange Country," "King of the Bingo Game," and "Flying Home," were written and published in 1944 while Ellison was serving in the merchant marine—only a year before he wrote the magical first sentence of *Invisible Man.*

The six stories unpublished in his lifetime—"A Party Down at the Square" (untitled by Ellison), "Boy on a Train," "Hymie's Bull," "I Did Not Learn Their Names," "A Hard Time Keeping Up" (also untitled), and "The Black Ball"—have more elusive chronologies. Except for "Hymie's Bull," Ellison failed to date these stories. Four of them—"A Party Down at the Square," "Boy on a Train," "I Did Not Learn Their Names," and "Hymie's Bull"—were in the folder with the frayed "Early Stories" label. (Of these, the final draft of "I Did Not Learn Their Names" has Ellison's 1940 address—25 Hamilton Terrace, New York City—written in black ink at the top of the first page. The impressions made by the typewriter keys are similar enough to suggest that the final versions of these stories, except for "Hymie's Bull," were typed in New York.) Two fragmentary sketches, called "Bartender" and "One Man's Woman," and a much-worked-over story, by turns melodramatic or flat, variously titled "One Who Was Waiting," "Goodnight Irene," and "Irene, Goodnight," were also in the "Early Stories" folder. Elsewhere in the papers I came across manuscripts of "A Hard Time Keeping Up" and "The Black Ball." Judging from the letterheads of the typescripts, these two stories were drafted, if not completely finished or revised, during Ellison's feverish months of writing in Dayton from late 1937 to April 1938, when he returned to support himself while writing by working on the New York Writers Project of the WPA, a job he stayed with until Angelo Herndon persuaded him to become managing editor of the *Negro Quarterly* in 1942.

I have not included "A Storm of Blizzard Proportions," a story that, like "In a Strange Country," Ellison wrote in 1944 and set in Wales while he was steaming across the North Atlantic on merchant-marine missions to the port of Swansea and other destinations. He wrote two drafts of the story in 1944, then apparently put it aside clipped to a long letter of praise and criticism from a friend, also dated 1944. "A Storm of Blizzard Proportions" has several reveries, influenced by Joyce and Hemingway, focused on Jack Johnson and, later, on the protagonist's (and Ellison's) autobiographical association of Wales with the Ohio landscape he came to love after his mother's death. Excluding the story was all the more painful because Ellison felt attached enough to list it among those he had toyed with collecting more than a decade before his death. I have left it out because, although compelling and suggestive of literary influences on Ellison, the parts of the story do not come together as a convincing whole.

Editing Ellison's stories, I found myself rehearsing the argument between Edmund Wilson and the Modern Language Association about the nature of posthumous editions. It should be clear that the current volume is emphatically a reader's edition, not intended to be a variorum or scholarly edition. In most cases the changes I have made to published and unpublished stories alike are silent, minor copyediting corrections. Exceptions are indicated by brackets in the text. For example, in "The Black Ball" I have inserted into the text of the story Ellison's note describing the little boy, and in the opening paragraph of "Hymie's Bull" I have restored from an earlier draft a sentence apparently unintentionally left out of what appears to be the story's final version. Finally, I have given two stories untitled by Ellison titles consisting of a phrase from each story's respective manuscript.

The present collection chronicles Ellison's discovery of *his* American theme. In technique and style, subject matter and milieu, the thirteen stories show the young writer's promise and possibility in the late thirties and his gradual ascent to maturity in the mid-forties when, unbeknownst to him, he was about to conceive *Invisible Man.* The sequence I have chosen follows the life Ellison knew and imagined from boyhood and youth in the twenties and early thirties to manhood in the late thirties and early forties. Different faces look out from the stories. Sometimes tolerance and a wary solidarity break through the color line, while on other occasions unspeakable acts of cruelty and violence disfigure the countenance of Ellison's America. The deceptive Jim Crow "normalcy" of the twenties is here; so are the jolt of the Depression and the opportunity and antagonism of black experience during the Second World War. Throughout the stories, Ellison experiments with narrative technique, point of view, and the impact of geography on personality. Reading them, one is initiated into the protean shapes and guises of black experience from about 1920 to about 1945. Ellison's fidelity to contemporary reality also enables him to etch timeless patterns on his work, often, as in "Flying Home," the archetype of a young man passing through loss and desolation "back in[to] the world of men again."

4.

In an undated, handwritten note at the bottom of a page from his novel in progress Ellison wrote "book of stories," then the words "story of lynching and airplane. Have Fanny look up." But I found no further mention of the untitled story I have called "A Party Down at the Square." Nevertheless, the story is a tour de force, not least, as Ellison remarked of Hemingway's techniques and effects, because telling it "presented its own difficulties of convention." By narrating a brutal lynching in the voice of a Cincinnati white boy visiting his uncle in Alabama, Ellison defies what he called in "Twentieth-Century Fiction and the Black Mask of Humanity" (1946) the "segregation of the word," and crosses the narrative color line then lingering in American literature. Like the black lynching victim, Ellison's white narrator is unnamed—doubtless, he covets anonymity. Yet everything seen, heard, smelled, touched, and felt while the black man is burning is expressed only in the feelings, words, and point of view of the boy watching.

As the writer, Ellison slips into the breaks and looks around under the skin of his young white narrator. The story is taut with the writer's restraint and the narrator's matter-of-fact, frightening, shameless account of the night. The boy speaks an idiom so unself-consciously reportorial that it becomes self-conscious. In his last words the boy tries to both declare and disguise his respect for the murdered man. "It was my first party and my last. God, but that nigger was tough. That Bacote nigger was some nigger!" The repetition of *nigger* denies, affirms, and again denies the mystery and equality of the human condition.

Ellison subtly plays off what he termed in "Brave Words for a Startling Occasion" that "mood of personal moral responsibility for democracy" he felt had all but disappeared from American literature after classic nineteenth-century fiction yielded to the moderns in the 1920s. In "A Party Down at the Square" he imagines a lynching from the perspective of someone without a moral point of view. His technique compels readers to experience the human condition in extremis, mediated by a stranger hell-bent only on observation and not the act of witness. Except for the black victim, the participants and spectators are white folks from near and far, titillated by the slow, excruciating torture of the "Bacote nigger"—for what crime or affront the narrator gives not the slightest hint; probably he does not know. Intriguingly, Ellison's words, almost fifty years later, in "An Extravagance of Laughter," on the ritual meaning of lynching seem a gloss on his early story: "Hence their deafness to cries of pain, their stoniness before the sight and stench of burning flesh, their exhilarated and grotesque self-righteousness." And things are exactly so. Presently, the onlookers in the story are horrified by the sizzling flesh of a woman electrocuted by a live wire knocked free by an airplane whose pilot, in the confusion and fury of a cyclone, mistakes the lynching's ring of fire for airport signal flares. But the lynchers' revulsion is brief; they turn back to the business at hand as if only the veritable end of the world could divert them from burning the black man alive.

The contrast between the human and natural aberrations of lynching and the cyclone is not remarked on by the narrator. His morality is a commitment to be noncommital, as if accuracy depended on neutrality. Ellison's readers must earn the right to be interpreters. For example, the narrator reveals the sheriff's presence only when he observes that he and "his men were yelling and driving folks back with guns shining in their hands"—driving them from the deadly live wires back toward the black man still roped to the fiery platform. It need not be said that the sheriff is using his good offices on behalf of the illegal lynching; the effect is conveyed by what Hemingway called "the sequence of motion and fact which made the emotion." As the action moves inexorably toward accomplishment of the ritual violence, the narrator's detachment becomes even more chilling, because he has no relation either to the "nigger" or to his own conscience. His sensibility is limited to the mere sensations of conditioned perception, his response so flat and one-dimensional it awakens the reader more keenly to what *is* taking place. Yet the young white witness testifies in metaphor about the impression left when the black man's pain is most indelible. "I'll never forget it. Every time I eat barbeque I'll remember that nigger. His back was just like a barbecued hog. I could see the prints of his ribs where they start around from his backbone and curve down and around. It was a sight to see, that nigger's back." But the boy's most *telling* response comes from his insides when, to his shame, he throws up. "I was sick, and tired, and weak, and cold." His sensations *are* his response, and they signify a resistance to the values he's been taught not to question. Afterward, the narrator says, "It blew for three days" and, in a reflex verbal action, gives recurring ambivalent testimony to the toughness of the murdered man. Beyond him, Ellison's sleight of hand leaves readers feeling that what has happened will not blow over in the aftermath of nature's storm—or man's.

"A Party Down at the Square" is an anomaly. Told by a white boy, the tale creates a stark background for Ellison's exploration of African-American life and character in the stories that follow. In between "A Party Down at the Square" and "Flying Home" ("'. . . they tell me I caused a storm and a coupla lynchings down here in Macon County,'" old black Jefferson says in his folktale within "Flying Home"), the stories follow Ellison's imagined trajectory of black experience from boyhood and youth to manhood. In contrast to "A Party Down at the Square," where fact and sensation threaten to overwhelm the whole of consciousness, the other stories depend on the characters' "conscientious consciousness." The young white narrator in "A Party Down at the Square" survives without probing the meaning of things; in this Alabama town the shallower his responses, the better he'll do. Not so Ellison's other narrators and characters. As black Americans, their lives depend on knowing both *what* it was all about and *how* to live in it.

In "Boy on a Train," James, who has recently lost his father, rides with his mother and baby brother from Oklahoma City to McAlester, where a job as a domestic awaits his mother. (Ellison, too, took such a journey with his mother and younger brother, Herbert, and spent a year in McAlester.) "Boy on a Train" centers reality in the family; the protagonist, young James, sees the world in terms of its impact on his immediate kin. In the story James veers back and forth between the things of boyhood and expectations that he act like the man he is not. With his child's eyes, he sees that white folks look differently at black people, wonders why, and, in the absence of an explanation, relies on wariness and alertness as camouflage against danger. His curiosity spurs him to learn the difference between how things looked (and were supposed to be) and how they are. He notices the difference between the world passing by the train window and conventional images of that world; the cow he sees looks "like a cow in the baby's picture book, only there were no butterflies about her head."

In the three early Buster-and-Riley stories, Ellison dramatizes his boyhood feeling—remembered in *Shadow and Act*—that "the fact that certain limitations had been imposed upon our freedom did not lessen our sense of obligation. Not only were we to prepare but we were to perform—not with mere competence but with an almost reckless verve, with, may we say (without evoking the quaint and questionable notion of *negritude*), Negro American style?" The two boys pursue what Ellison calls "the performance of many and diverse roles" in their longing to escape from the confining though protective nests of family, and fly freely in the larger world.

In "Mister Toussan," Buster and Riley improvise a tall-tale version of Toussaint L'Ouverture's historical exploits in the manner of call-and-response until the symbolic action of their language emboldens them to plot sneaking after some cherries that white man Rogan has declared off-limits. So it goes in "Afternoon" as the boys chafe at the dead-end combination of boredom and conflicts with their elders in which race raises the ante. Riley's father threatens to "smoke him," in restoration of the old slave-borne punishment, and Buster resents his mother's irritability all the more for knowing it came on "whenever something went wrong with her and the white folks." In "That I Had the Wings," when churchgoing elder Aunt Kate silences Riley's signifying riffs on the Lord's name and the Jim Crow code, the boys test their curiosity and restless aspiration against the limitations of nature. But when their scheme to teach some baby chicks to fly kills the chicks, Aunt Kate reappears like the angel of death, and Buster and Riley settle for the flight of words.

"A Coupla Scalped Indians" tells of a rite of passage in a narrative style that gives experience the quality of both immediacy and retrospection. When the boys hear the nasty mouth, signifying trumpet, as they walk toward the carnival from far off in the woods, Buster improvises words to go with what he hears in the music's free flight:

> "Saying,
>
> *'So ya'll don't play 'em, hey?*
> *So ya'll won't play 'em, hey?*
> *Well pat your feet and clap your hands,*
> *'Cause I'm going to play 'em to the promised land.*
>
> "Man, the white folks know what that fool is signifying on that horn they'd run him clear on out the world."

But it's the narrator who, recently "scalped" (circumcised) like Buster, blunders into knowledge in the tabooed shack of old Aunt Mackie for which others might run him "out the world." Dazed, he emerges from his ambiguous, solitary manchild's encounter with this ancient woman, mysterious and magical as the moon, whose naked body belies her wrinkled face with its telltale hairs and tenders him the promise and beauty of youth and the tidal pull of sexuality. "All is real," he confides in wonder. Alone in the night, his sharpened senses touched by the shapes of nature, the narrator's nuanced sensibility becomes suddenly attuned to feelings that open him to the mystery and possibility of life and the world.

"Hymie's Bull" and its companion story, "I Did Not Learn Their Names," are fictions of wariness, violence, and a surprising tenderness. Both stories refigure Ellison's experiences hoboing the freights in the early thirties. "Hymie's Bull" follows an unnamed young man on his own, on the road, going nowhere like others of his age; and in "I Did Not Learn Their Names," another unnamed young man is hoboing his way *somewhere*—to college in Alabama, as Ellison did the summer of 1933. In each story the narration begins in the first-person plural, as if riding the rails gave the down-and-out a fraternal bond like that enjoyed by a ship's crew. In "Hymie's Bull" the *we* persists from beginning to end, punctuated by occasional shifts to *you* as Ellison's narrator reaches out to those listening, and *I* when he bears witness to the bull's unprovoked attack on Hymie and Hymie's killing of the bull with a knife. In the eyes of Ellison's narrator, Hymie is a matador, his suddenly unfurled knife a muleta. "Hymie's Bull" becomes an escape story, too, for the young black narrator and his companions are due for a beating, jailing, or worse when they're lined up in the Montgomery yards by two Alabama bulls snorting to avenge their dead fellow. The young hoboes are "happy as hell" riding on top of the freight car carrying them far away from the scene of the killing and the nearby Scottsboro frame-up of a couple of years before.

"I Did Not Learn Their Names" begins as if the narrator of "Hymie's Bull," more experienced now, tells another story. Here, *we* refers to the narrator and his buddy, and soon becomes *I* as he tells of Morrie, a white guy with an artificial leg, saving him from falling between two cars. Like "Hymie's Bull," "I Did Not Learn Their Names" moves in the syncopated rhythm of the freights its narrator rides, sometimes smoothly and swiftly, sometimes with the herky-jerky motion of cars bumping along, coupling and uncoupling in sudden stops, then returning to crawl or race toward a destination somewhere that is also nowhere. Like his successor Invisible Man, the narrator is personal, even intimate. "I was having a hard time trying not to hate in those days," he confesses, and follows with a well-honed response to racial prejudice. "I still fought the bums—with Morrie's help. But I had learned not to attack those who were not personally aggressive and who only expressed passively what they had been taught." The young man vividly evokes the countryside from Colorado back through Kansas to Oklahoma, perhaps as Ellison remembered it from a trip to Denver with his high school band. At any rate, the old married couple the narrator meets in a boxcar are touching to each other and kind to him, almost to a fault. Keeping to the anonymity of "Hymie's Bull," the narrator does not identify himself. But he acknowledges the complexity of knowledge and language, revealing that he learned about Scottsboro while a prisoner in Decatur, Alabama, and that "I thought of the old couple often during those days I lay in jail, and I was sorry that I had not learned their names." He had, of course, learned more than that. Once again there is Ellison's (and his characters') hunger for democratic equality; like Twain's raft and Melville's whaling ship, Ellison's rails open up possibilities of fraternity even in the face of violence, danger, and racial hatred.

"A Hard Time Keeping Up," "The Black Ball," and "King of the Bingo Game" are stories of young black men testing the ground under their feet in the larger world, adapting to life as a game of chance in which the odds are long, the outcome at best in doubt and at worst fixed, even when you've won the jackpot. Like the trolley rail covered by snow in "A Hard Time Keeping Up," the color line is always there. Visible or invisible, it's palpable to the two dining-car waiters laying over in an unidentified town not that far from the Mason-Dixon Line and to John, the caretaker and handyman for an apartment building in "The Black Ball." Like other early unpublished stories, "A Hard Time Keeping Up" is told by a narrator unidentified except for a fleeting reference to "Al" by his friend Joe, who seethes at the Jim Crow scheme of things, often on the verge of rage. The story gives the feel of two guys tramping through the snow to the best rooming house on the Negro side of town. They don't look for trouble, but they expect it. Yet when what appears to be an ugly, sexually charged racial incident turns out to be a friendly wager between the underworld character, Ike, and Charlie, his black acquaintance from the sporting world, Joe and Al have the resiliency to laugh. In a reverberation of Hemingway, Ellison turns the utterly flat danger and despair of "The Killers" inside out.

Games and stacked decks are apt metaphors for Jim Crow rules in "The Black Ball," perhaps the most subtly crafted and realized of the unpublished stories. John, the narrator, is taut with a father's tenderness for his son. He is aware that no matter what he does, the boy will have—indeed, already has begun to have—his initiation into "the old ball game" of crooked ground rules. Set in the Southwest and, like other unpublished stories, typed on the back of the letterhead of the Montgomery County Republican Executive Committee, "The Black Ball" is nuanced by the narrator's sensitivity to differences between the South and the Southwest. "Doesn't he know we aren't afraid to fight his kind out this way?" John wonders in a reflex response to the stereotype of the redneck before he learns that the man's hands were fried with a gasoline torch because he stuck to his alibi for a black friend falsely accused of raping a white woman back in Alabama. Hearing the story and seeing the man's hands, John feels his suspicion ebb. Here and elsewhere in the early stories, Ellison's African-American characters show a persistent willingness to overcome their hostility to whites, suspend their disbelief, and perhaps join efforts toward brotherhood, in this case a union trying to organize black and white building-service workers. John's memory of the white organizer's burned hands, together with his boss's threat to put him behind the black ball and his little boy's wise-fool's questions, nudges him toward the thought that "maybe there was a color other than white on the old ball."

"King of the Bingo Game" is a third-person story in which a greenhorn migrant from the South to Harlem draws bingo and the right to take a turn at the wheel of fortune and the jackpot. Despite his urgent need for money to secure medical help for his wife, the act of spinning the wheel becomes his energy, his life, his God. The King of Bingo experiences that demonic power that Leon Forrest, in his "Luminosity from the Lower Frequencies," associates with Ellison's defiant imagination. He feels so liberated by the act of pressing the button that he cannot let go until it is forcibly taken from him by security cops, one of whom blackjacks him at the same moment he sees the wheel stop at double zero and the jackpot. Double zero is his fate; it's "winner take nothing" except a beating behind the curtain, and doubtless again in jail or in the gutter before he's set free. "King of the Bingo Game" anticipates the tithe paid to fluidity, violence, chaos, and the surreal throughout *Invisible Man.*

In its concentration on the riddle of identity, "In a Strange Country" also anticipates *Invisible Man.* In this story, "the answer to the complicated question of identity is a musical one," Robert G. O'Meally has observed in *The Craft of Ralph Ellison,* and "music, here, is Ellison's metaphor for democracy and love." In his aching self-consciousness, the protagonist Parker realizes that to the Welshmen who befriended him after his fellow Yank servicemen blackened his eye, *he* is the true American. They recognize, as Ellison wrote many years later, that there is "something indisputably American about Negroes." How painful it is for Parker to recognize and act on this perception. While the Welsh chorus belts out "The Star-Spangled Banner," "as though to betray him he heard his own voice singing out like a suddenly amplified radio." In the subconscious, the "strange country" stands less for Wales than for America, and like many Americans, Parker discovers his Americanness overseas. Attacked without provocation by the first white fellow countrymen he sees in Wales, Parker feels ambivalence toward America as both "the horrible foreboding country of dreams" and the country whose ideals he experienced in mixed jam sessions back home. "When we jam, sir, we're Jamocrats," he thinks to himself. Asked "HOW DOES IT FEEL TO BE FREE OF ILLUSION?" Invisible Man will reply: "Painful and empty." And earlier, in "In a Strange Country," Parker lays claims to an America "free of illusion." His struggle for self-definition foreshadows Ellison's desire, expressed in his 1981 Introduction to the thirtieth-anniversary edition of *Invisible Man,* "to create a narrator who could think as well as act" and whose "capacity for conscious self-assertion" was "basic to his blundering quest for freedom." Like other narrators and characters in these stories, Parker anticipates Ellison's creation, in *Invisible Man,* of "a blues-toned laugher at wounds who included himself in his indictment of the human condition," and was therefore better able to see and embrace the world in its diversity.

Along with "A Party Down at the Square," "Flying Home" frames the collection. The tale anticipates invisibility, the grandfather's riddle, and the technique of solos and breaks with which Ellison took such flight in *Invisible Man.* In

"Flying Home," just when Ellison's northern protagonist believes, with a nod to Joyce's Stephen Dedalus, that he has learned to use his wiles to escape the limitations of race, language, and geography, circumstances force him to confront the strange "old country" of the South. A literary descendant of Icarus, Todd, one of the black eagles from the Negro air school at Tuskegee, flies too close to the sun and falls to earth in rural Alabama. There, unlike his mythological forebear, he is saved by Jefferson, whose folktales and actions enable Todd to recognize where he is and who he is, and to come back to life by following the old black peasant and his son out of a labyrinthine Alabama valley. Laughter, which Todd earlier associates with humiliation, erupts from deep inside him at the story's climax, and taking advantage of the chaos, old Jefferson comes to the rescue and bears him away from danger.

In the 1981 Introduction to *Invisible Man,* Ellison recalls his pilot as a "man of two worlds," who "felt himself to be misperceived in both, and thus was at ease in neither." Looking ahead, he concludes that "I by no means was aware of his relationship to the invisible man, but clearly he possessed some of the symptoms." And, Ellison might have added, he possessed a share of Invisible Man's eventual, qualified, fraternal, democratic optimism. "A new current of communication [that] flowed between the man and boy and himself" enables Todd to transfigure a buzzard—one of the "jimcrows" he'd feared, identified with, and flown into on a training flight—into an emblem of flight and freedom. In the story's last words he "saw the dark bird glide into the sun and glow like a bird of flaming gold," perhaps a prophetic image, inspired by Lionel Hampton's high-velocity signature jazz tune, "Flying Home," of Ellison's triumphant soaring in *Invisible Man.*

5.

Taken together, the short stories point to Ellison's remarkably consistent vision of American identity over the fifty-five years of his writing life. In "The Black Ball" the little boy asks his father a question others before him have asked and those who have come after still ask from different sides of the color line. "Brown's much nicer than white, isn't it, Daddy?" "Some people think so," his father concedes. "But American is better than both, son." His response asserts Ellison's belief in a common—*not identical, but common*—democratic identity. Simply put, this sentiment is Ellison's creed. Like the narrator of this long-ago story, he pledges allegiance to America and the ideal for which it stands, aware of the distance that persists between the country's reality and its principle. For Ellison, the idea of America is first cousin to the possibilities of fiction. He considered each a territory, as he inscribed in a friend's book, "ever to be sought, ever to be missed, but always there." Of his short stories this much we can say: They led Ralph Ellison into the territory of the novel—toward *Invisible Man,* with its freighted, frightening, fraternal "lower frequencies" of democracy, and beyond, to the terra incognita of his novel in progress.

—John F. Callahan
Washington, D.C.
November 1996

FLYING HOME
and Other Stories

A Party Down at the Square

I don't know what started it. A bunch of men came by my Uncle Ed's place and said there was going to be a party down at the Square, and my uncle hollered for me to come on and I ran with them through the dark and rain and there we were at the Square. When we got there everybody was mad and quiet and standing around looking at the nigger. Some of the men had guns, and one man kept goosing the nigger in his pants with the barrel of a shotgun, saying he ought to pull the trigger, but he never did. It was right in front of the courthouse, and the old clock in the tower was striking twelve. The rain was falling cold and freezing as it fell. Everybody was cold, and the nigger kept wrapping his arms around himself trying to stop the shivers.

Then one of the boys pushed through the circle and

snatched off the nigger's shirt, and there he stood, with his black skin all shivering in the light from the fire, and looking at us with a scaired look on his face and putting his hands in his pants pockets. Folks started yelling to hurry up and kill the nigger. Somebody yelled: "Take your hands out of your pockets, nigger; we gonna have plenty heat in a minnit." But the nigger didn't hear him and kept his hands where they were.

I tell you the rain was cold. I had to stick my hands in my pockets they got so cold. The fire was pretty small, and they put some logs around the platform they had the nigger on and then threw on some gasoline, and you could see the flames light up the whole Square. It was late and the streetlights had been off for a long time. It was so bright that the bronze statue of the general standing there in the Square was like something alive. The shadows playing on his moldy green face made him seem to be smiling down at the nigger.

They threw on more gas, and it made the Square bright like it gets when the lights are turned on or when the sun is setting red. All the wagons and cars were standing around the curbs. Not like Saturday though—the niggers weren't there. Not a single nigger was there except this Bacote nigger and they dragged him there tied to the back of Jed Wilson's truck. On Saturday there's as many niggers as white folks.

Everybody was yelling crazy 'cause they were about to set fire to the nigger, and I got to the rear of the circle and looked around the Square to try to count the cars. The shadows of the folks was flickering on the trees in the middle of the Square. I saw some birds that the noise had woke up flying through the trees. I guess maybe they thought it was morning. The ice had started the cobblestones in the street to shine where the rain was falling and freezing. I counted forty cars before I lost count. I knew folks must have been there from Phenix City by all the cars mixed in with the wagons.

God, it was a hell of a night. It was some night all right. When the noise died down I heard the nigger's voice from where I stood in the back, so I pushed my way up front. The nigger was bleeding from his nose and ears, and I could see him all red where the dark blood was running down his black skin. He kept lifting first one foot and then the other, like a chicken on a hot stove. I looked down to the platform they had him on, and they had pushed a ring of fire up close to his feet. It must have been hot to him with the flames almost touching his big black toes. Somebody yelled for the nigger to say his prayers, but the nigger wasn't saying anything now. He just kinda moaned with his eyes shut and kept moving up and down on his feet, first one foot and then the other.

I watched the flames burning the logs up closer and closer to the nigger's feet. They were burning good now, and the rain had stopped and the wind was rising, making the flames flare higher. I looked, and there must have been thirty-five women in the crowd, and I could hear their voices clear and shrill mixed in with those of the men. Then it happened. I heard the noise about the same time everyone else did. It was like the roar of a cyclone blowing up from the gulf, and everyone was looking up into the air to see what it was. Some of the faces looked surprised and scaired, all but the nigger. He didn't even hear the noise. He didn't even look up. Then the roar came closer, right above our heads and the wind was blowing higher and higher and the sound seemed to be going in circles.

Then I saw her. Through the clouds and fog I could see a red and green light on her wings. I could see them just for a second; then she rose up into the low clouds. I looked out for the beacon over the tops of the buildings in the direction of the airfield that's forty miles away, and it wasn't circling around. You usually could see it sweeping around the sky at night, but it wasn't there. Then, there she was again, like a big bird lost in the fog. I looked for the red and green lights, and they weren't there anymore. She was flying even closer to the tops of the buildings than before. The wind was blowing harder, and leaves started flying about, making funny shadows on the ground, and tree limbs were cracking and falling.

It was a storm all right. The pilot must have thought he was over the landing field. Maybe he thought the fire in the Square was put there for him to land by. Gosh, but it scaired the folks. I was scaired too. They started yelling: "He's going to land. He's going to land." And: "He's going to fall." A few started for their cars and wagons. I could hear the wagons creaking and chains jangling and cars spitting and missing as they started the engines up. Off to my right, a horse started pitching and striking his hooves against a car.

I didn't know what to do. I wanted to run, and I wanted to stay and see what was going to happen. The plane was close as hell. The pilot must have been trying to see where he was at, and her motors were drowning out all the sounds. I could even feel the vibration, and my hair felt like it was standing up under my hat. I happened to look over at the statue of the general standing with one leg before the other and leaning back on a sword, and I was fixing to run over and climb between his legs and sit there and watch when the roar stopped some, and I looked up and she was gliding just over the top of the trees in the middle of the Square.

Her motors stopped altogether and I could hear the sound of branches cracking and snapping off below her landing gear. I could see her plain now, all silver and shining in the light of the fire with T.W.A. in black letters under her wings. She was sailing smoothly out of the Square when she hit the high power lines that follow the Birmingham highway through the town. It made a loud crash. It sounded like the wind blowing the door of a tin barn shut. She only hit with her landing gear, but I could see the sparks flying, and the wires knocked loose from the poles were spitting blue sparks and whipping around like a bunch of snakes and leaving circles of blue sparks in the darkness.

The plane had knocked five or six wires loose, and they were dangling and swinging, and every time they touched they threw off more sparks. The wind was making them swing, and when I got over there, there was a crackling and spitting screen of blue haze across the highway. I lost my hat running over, but I didn't stop to look for it. I was among the first and I could hear the others pounding behind me across the grass of the Square. They were yelling to beat all hell, and they came up fast, pushing and shoving, and someone got pushed against a swinging wire. It made a sound like when a blacksmith drops a red hot horseshoe into a barrel of water, and the steam comes up. I could smell the flesh burning. The first time I'd ever smelled it. I got up close and it was a woman. It must have killed her right off. She was lying in a puddle stiff as a board, with pieces of glass insulators that the plane had knocked off the poles lying all around her. Her white dress was torn, and I saw one of her tits hanging out in the water and her thighs. Some woman screamed and fainted and almost fell on a wire, but a man caught her. The sheriff and his men were yelling and driving folks back with guns shining in their hands, and everything was lit up blue by the sparks. The shock had turned the woman almost as black as the nigger.

I was trying to see if she wasn't blue too, or if it was just the sparks, and the sheriff drove me away. As I backed off trying to see, I heard the motors of the plane start up again somewhere off to the right in the clouds.

The clouds were moving fast in the wind and the wind was blowing the smell of something burning over to me. I turned around, and the crowd was headed back to the nigger. I could see him standing there in the middle of the flames. The wind was making the flames brighter every minute. The crowd was running. I ran too. I ran back across the grass with the crowd. It wasn't so large now that so many had gone when the plane came. I tripped and fell over the limb of a tree lying in the grass and bit my lip. It ain't well yet I bit it so bad. I could taste the blood in my mouth as I ran over. I guess that's what made me sick. When I got there, the fire had caught the nigger's pants, and the folks were standing around watching, but not too close on account of the wind blowing the flames. Somebody hollered, "Well, nigger, it ain't so cold now, is it? You don't need to put your hands in your pockets now." And the nigger looked up with his great white eyes looking like they was 'bout to pop out of his head, and I had enough. I didn't want to see anymore. I wanted to run somewhere and puke, but I stayed. I stayed right there in the front of the crowd and looked.

The nigger tried to say something I couldn't hear for the roar of the wind in the fire, and I strained my ears. Jed Wilson hollered, "What you say there, nigger?" And it came back through the flames in his nigger voice: "Will one a you gentlemen please cut my throat?" he said. "Will somebody please cut my throat like a Christian?" And Jed hollered back, "Sorry, but ain't no Christians around tonight. Ain't no Jew-boys neither. We're just one hundred percent Americans."

Then the nigger was silent. Folks started laughing at Jed. Jed's right popular with the folks, and next year, my uncle says, they plan to run him for sheriff. The heat was too much for me, and the smoke was making my eyes to smart. I was trying to back away when Jed reached down and brought up a can of gasoline and threw it in the fire on the nigger. I could see the flames catching the gas in a puff as it went in in a silver sheet and some of it reached the nigger, making spurts of blue fire all over his chest.

Well, that nigger was tough. I have to give it to that nigger; he was really tough. He had started to burn like a house afire and was making the smoke smell like burning hides. The fire was up around his head, and the smoke was so thick and black we couldn't see him. And him not moving—we thought he was dead. Then he started out. The fire had burned the ropes they had tied him with, and he started jumping and kicking about like he was blind, and you could smell his skin burning. He kicked so hard that the platform, which was burning too, fell in, and he rolled out of the fire at my feet. I jumped back so he wouldn't get on me. I'll never forget it. Every time I eat barbeque I'll remember that nigger. His back was just like a barbecued hog. I could see the prints of his ribs where they start around from his backbone and curve down and around. It was a sight to see, that nigger's back. He was right at my feet, and somebody behind pushed me and almost made me step on him, and he was still burning.

I didn't step on him though, and Jed and somebody else pushed him back into the burning planks and logs and poured on more gas. I wanted to leave, but the folks were yelling and I couldn't move except to look around and see the statue. A branch the wind had broken was resting on his hat. I tried to push out and get away because my guts were gone, and all I got was spit and hot breath in my face from the woman and two men standing directly behind me. So I had to turn back around. The nigger rolled out of the fire again. He wouldn't stay put. It was on the other side this time. I couldn't see him very well through the flames and smoke. They got some tree limbs and held him there this time and he stayed there till he was ashes. I guess he stayed there. I know he burned to ashes because I saw Jed a week later, and he laughed and showed me some white finger bones still held together with little pieces of the nigger's skin. Anyway, I left when somebody moved around to see the nigger. I pushed my way through the crowd, and a woman in the rear scratched my face as she yelled and fought to get up close.

I ran across the Square to the other side, where the sheriff and his deputies were guarding the wires that were still spitting and making a blue fog. My heart was pounding like I had been running a long ways, and I bent over and let my insides go. Everything came up and spilled in a big gush over the ground. I was sick, and tired, and weak, and cold. The wind was still high, and large drops of rain were beginning to fall. I headed down the street to my uncle's place past a store where the wind had broken a window, and glass lay over the sidewalk. I kicked it as I went by. I remember somebody's fool rooster crowing like it was morning in all that wind.

The next day I was too weak to go out, and my uncle kidded me and called me "the gutless wonder from Cincinnati." I didn't mind. He said you get used to it in time. He couldn't go out hisself. There was too much wind and rain. I got up and looked out of the window, and the rain was pouring down and dead sparrows and limbs of trees were scattered all over the yard. There had been a cyclone all right. It swept a path right through the county, and we were lucky we didn't get the full force of it.

It blew for three days steady, and put the town in a hell of a shape. The wind blew sparks and set fire to the white-and-green-trimmed house on Jackson Avenue that had the big concrete lions in the yard and burned it down to the ground. They had to kill another nigger who tried to run out of the county after they burned this Bacote nigger. My Uncle Ed said they always have to kill niggers in pairs to keep the other niggers in place. I don't know though, the folks seem a little skittish of the niggers. They all came back, but they act pretty sullen. They look mean as hell when you pass them down at the store. The other day I was down to Brinkley's store, and a white cropper said it didn't do no good to kill the niggers 'cause things don't get no better. He looked hungry as hell. Most of the croppers look hungry. You'd be surprised how hungry white folks can look. Somebody said that he'd better shut his damn mouth, and he shut up. But from the look on his face he won't stay shut long. He went out of the store muttering to himself and spit a big chew of tobacco right down on Brinkley's floor. Brinkley said he was sore 'cause he wouldn't let him have credit. Anyway, it didn't seem to help things. First it was the nigger and the storm, then the plane, then the woman and the wires, and now I hear the airplane line is investigating to find who set the fire that almost wrecked their plane. All that in one night, and all of it but the storm over one nigger. It was some night all right. It was some party too. I was right there, see. I was right there watching it all. It was my first party and my last. God, but that nigger was tough. That Bacote nigger was some nigger!

Boy on a Train

The train gave a long, shrill, lonely whistle, and seemed to gain speed as it rushed downgrade between two hills covered with trees. The trees were covered with deep-red, brown, and yellow leaves. The leaves fell on the side of the hill and scattered down to the gray rocks along the opposite tracks. When the engine blew off steam, the little boys could see the white cloud scatter the colored leaves against the side of the hill. The engine hissed, and the leaves danced in the steam like leaves in a white wind.

"See, Lewis, Jack Frost made the pretty leaves. Jack Frost paints the leaves all the pretty colors. See, Lewis: brown, and purple, and orange, and yellow."

From *The New Yorker,* April 29 & May 6, 1996

The little boy pointed and paused after naming each color, his finger bent against the glass of the train window. The baby repeated the colors after him, looking intently for Jack Frost.

It was hot in the train, and the car was too close to the engine, making it impossible to open the window. More than once, cinders found a way into the car and flew into the baby's eyes. The woman raised her head from her book from time to time to watch the little boys. The car was filthy, and part of it was used for baggage. Up front, the pine shipping box of a casket stood in a corner. Wonder what poor soul that is in there, the woman thought.

Bags and trunks covered the floor up front, and now and then the butcher came in to pick up candy, or fruit or magazines, to sell back in the white cars. He would come in and pick up a basket with candy, go out, come back; pick up a basket of fruit, go out; come back, pick up magazines, and on till everything had been carried out; then he would start all over again.

He was a big, fat white man with a red face, and the little boy hoped he would give them a piece of candy; after all, he had so much, and Mama didn't have any nickels to give them. But he never did.

The mother read intently, holding a page in her hand as she scanned, then turned it slowly. They were the only passengers in the section of seats reserved for colored. She turned her head, looking back toward the door leading to the other car; it was time for the butcher to return. Her brow wrinkled annoyedly. The butcher had tried to touch her breasts when she and the boys first came into the car, and she had spat in his face and told him to keep his dirty hands where they belonged. The butcher had turned red and gone hurriedly out of the car, his baskets swinging violently on his arms. She hated him. Why couldn't a Negro woman travel with her two boys without being molested?

The train was past the hills now, and into fields that were divided by crooked wooden fences and that spread rolling and brown with stacks of corn as far as the blue horizon fringed with trees. The fences reminded the boy of the crooked man who walked a crooked mile.

Red birds darted swiftly past the car, ducking down into the field, then shooting up again when you looked back to see the telephone poles and fields turning, and sliding fast away from the train. The boys were having a good time of it. It was their first trip. The countryside was bright gold with Indian summer. Way across a field, a boy was leading a cow by a rope and a dog was barking at the cow's feet. It was a nice dog, the boy on the train thought, a collie. Yes, that was the kind of dog it was—a collie.

A freight was passing, going in the direction of Oklahoma City, passing so swiftly that its orange-and-red cars seemed a streak of watercolor with gray spaces punched through. The boy felt funny whenever he thought of Oklahoma City, like he wanted to cry. Perhaps they would never go back. He wondered what Frank and R.C. and Petey were doing now. Picking peaches for Mr. Stewart? A lump rose in his throat. Too bad they had to leave just when Mr. Stewart had promised them half of all the peaches they could pick. He sighed. The train whistle sounded very sad and lonesome.

Well, now they were going to McAlester, where Mama would have a nice job and enough money to pay the bills. Gee, Mama must have been a good worker for Mr. Balinger to send all the way to Oklahoma City for her to come work for him. Mama was happy to go, and he was glad for Mama to be happy; she worked so hard now that Daddy was gone. He closed his eyes tight, trying to see the picture of Daddy. He must never forget how Daddy looked. He would look like that himself when he grew up: tall and kind and always joking and reading books. . . . *Well, just wait; when he got big and carried Mama and Lewis back to Oklahoma City everybody would see how well he took care of Mama, and she would say, "See, these are my two boys," and would be very proud. And everybody would say, "See, aren't Mrs. Weaver's boys two fine men?" That was the way it would be.*

The thought made him lose some of the lump that came into his throat when he thought of never, never going back, and he turned to see who it was coming through the door.

A white man and a little boy came into the car and walked up front. His mother looked up, then lowered her eyes to her book again. He stood up and looked over the backs of the chairs, trying to see what the man and boy were doing. The white boy held a tiny dog in his arms, stroking its head. The little white boy asked the man to let him take the dog out, but the man said no, and they went, rocking from side to side, out of the car. The dog must have been asleep, because all the time he hadn't made a sound. The little white boy was dressed like the kids you see in moving pictures. Did he have a bike? the boy wondered.

He looked out the window. There were horses now, a herd of them, running and tossing their manes and tails and pounding the ground all wild when the whistle blew. He saw himself on a white horse, swinging a l-a-r-i-a-t over the broncos' heads and yelling "Yip, yip, yippee!" like Hoot Gibson in the movies. The horses excited Lewis, and he beat his hands against the window and cried, "Giddap! Giddap!" The boy smiled and looked at his mother. She was looking up from her page and smiling, too. Lewis was cute, he thought.

They stopped at a country town. Men were standing in front of the station, watching the porter throw off a bunch of newspapers. Then several white men came into the car and one said, "This must be it," and pointed to the big box, and the porter said, "Yeah, this is it all right. It's the only one we got this trip, so this must be the one." Then the porter jumped out of the car and went into the station. The men were dressed in black suits with white shirts. They seemed very uncomfortable with their high collars, and acted very solemn. They pushed the box over gently and lifted it out the side door of the car. The white men in overalls watched them from the platform. They put the box in a wagon, and the man said "Giddap" to the horses and they drove away, the men on the back with the box looking very straight and stiff.

One of the men on the platform was picking his teeth and spitting tobacco juice on the ground. The station was painted green, and a sign on the side read TUBE ROSE SNUFF and showed a big white flower; it didn't look like a rose, though. It was hot, and the men had their shirts open at the collar and wore red bandannas around their necks. They were standing in the same position when the train pulled out, staring. Why, he wondered, did white folks stare at you that way?

Outside the town, he saw a big red rock barn standing behind some trees. Beside it stood something he had never seen before. It was high and round and made out of the same kind of rock as the barn. He climbed into his seat and pointed.

"What is that tall thing, Mama?" he said.

She raised her head and looked.

"It's a silo, son," she said. "That's where the corn is stored." Her eyes were strangely distant when she turned her face back to him. The sun slanted across her eyes, and her skin was brown and clear. He eased down into the seat. *Silo, silo. Almost as tall as the Colcord Building in Oklahoma City that Daddy helped to build . . .*

He jumped, startled; Mama was calling his name with tears in her voice. He turned around and tears were on her face.

"Come around here, James," she said. "Bring Lewis."

He took Lewis by the hand and moved into the seat beside her. *What had they done?*

"James, son," she said. "That old silo back there's been here a long time. It made me remember when years ago me and your daddy came over this same old Rock Island line on our way to Oklahoma City. We had just been married and was very happy going west because we had heard that colored people had a chance out here."

James smiled, listening; he loved to hear Mama tell about when she and Daddy were young, and about what they used to do down South. Yet he felt this was to be something different. Something in Mama's voice was vast and high, like a rainbow; yet something sad and deep, like when the organ played in church, was around Mama's words.

"Son, I want you to remember this trip," she said. "You

understand, son. I *want* you to remember. You *must,* you've *got* to understand."

James sensed something; he tried hard to understand. He stared into her face. Tears were glistening in her eyes, and he felt he would cry himself. He bit his lip. No, he was the man of the family, and he couldn't act like the baby. He swallowed, listening.

"You remember this, James," she said. "We came all the way from Georgia on this same railroad line fourteen years ago, so things would be better for you children when you came. You must remember this, James. We traveled far, looking for a better world, where things wouldn't be so hard like they were down South. That was fourteen years ago, James. Now your father's gone from us, and you're the man. Things are hard for us colored folks, son, and it's just us three alone and we have to stick together. Things is hard, and we have to fight. . . . O Lord, we have to fight! . . ."

She stopped, her lips pressed tight together as she shook her head, overcome with emotion. James placed his arm around her neck and caressed her cheek.

"Yes, Mama," he said. "I won't forget."

He could not get it all, but yet he understood. It was like understanding what music without words said. He felt very full inside. Now Mama was pulling him close to her; the baby rested against her other side. This was familiar; since Daddy died Mama prayed with them, and now she was beginning to pray. He bowed his head.

"Go with us and keep us, Lord. Then it was me and him, Lord; now it's me and his children. And I'm thankful, Lord. You saw fit to take him, Lord, and it's well with my soul in Thy name. I was happy, Lord; life was like a mockingbird a-singing. And all I ask now is to stay with these children, to raise them and protect them, Lord, till they're old enough to go their way. Make them strong and unafraid, Lord. Give them strength to meet this world. Make them brave to go where things is better for our people, Lord. . . ."

James sat with head bowed. Always when Mama prayed, he felt tight and smoldering inside. And he kept remembering his father's face. He could not remember Daddy ever praying, but Daddy's voice had been deep and strong when he sang in the choir on Sunday mornings. James wanted to cry, but, vaguely, he felt *something* should be punished for making Mama cry. Something cruel had made her cry. He felt the tightness in his throat becoming anger. If he only knew what it was, he would fix it; he would kill this mean thing that made Mama feel so bad. It must have been awful because Mama was strong and brave and even killed mice when the white woman she used to work for only raised her dress and squealed like a girl, afraid of them. If he only knew what it was . . . Was it God?

"Please keep us three together in this strange town, Lord. The road is dark and long and my sorrows heavy but, if it be Thy will, Lord, let me educate my boys. Let me raise them so they'll be better able to live this life. I don't want to live for myself, Lord, just for these boys. Make them strong, upright men, Lord; make them fighters. And when my work on earth is done, take me home to Thy kingdom, Lord, safe in the arms of Jesus."

He heard her voice trail off to a tortured moan behind her trembling lips. Tears streamed down her face. James was miserable; he did not like to see Mama cry, and turned his eyes to the window as she began wiping away the tears. He was glad she was through now because the butcher would be coming back into the car in a few minutes. He did not want a white man to see Mama cry.

They were crossing a river now. The slanting girders of a bridge moved slowly past the train. The river was muddy and red, rushing along beneath them. The train stopped, and the baby was pointing to a cow on the banks of the river below. The cow stood gazing out over the water, chewing her cud—looking like a cow in the baby's picture book, only there were no butterflies about her head.

"Bow-wow!" the baby said. Then, questioningly: "Bow-wow?"

"No, Lewis, it's a cow," James said. "Moo," he said. "Cow." The baby laughed, delighted. "Moo-oo." He was very interested.

James watched the water. The train was moving again, and he wondered why his mother cried. It wasn't just that Daddy was gone; it didn't sound just that way. It was something else. I'll kill it when I get big, he thought. I'll make it cry just like it's making Mama cry!

The train was passing an oil field. There were many wells in the field; and big round tanks, gleaming like silver in the sun. One well was covered with boards and looked like a huge Indian wigwam against the sky. The wells all pointed straight up at the sky. Yes, I'll kill it. I'll make it cry. Even if it's God, I'll make God cry, he thought. I'll kill Him; I'll kill God and not be sorry!

The train jerked, gaining speed, and the wheels began clicking a ragged rhythm to his ears. There were many advertising signs in the fields they were rolling past. All the signs told about the same things for sale. One sign showed a big red bull and read BULL DURHAM.

"Moo-oo," the baby said.

James looked at his mother; she was through crying now, and she smiled. He felt some of his tightness ebb away. He grinned. He wanted very much to kiss her, but he must show the proper reserve of a man now. He grinned. Mama was beautiful when she smiled. He made a wish never to forget what she had said. "This is 1924, and I'll never forget it," he whispered to himself. Then he looked out the window, resting his chin on the palm of his hand, wondering how much farther they would have to ride, and if there would be any boys to play football in McAlester.

Mister Toussan

Once upon a time
The goose drink wine
Monkey chew tobacco
And he spit white lime

—Rhyme used as a prologue to Negro slave stories

"I hope they all gits rotten and the worms git in 'em," the first boy said.

"I hopes a big wind storm comes and blows down all the trees," said the second boy.

"Me too," the first boy said. "And when ole Rogan comes out to see what happened I hope a tree falls on his head and kills him."

"Now jus look a-yonder at them birds," the second boy said. "They eating all they want and when we asked him to let us git some off the ground he had to come calling us little nigguhs and chasing us home!"

From *New Masses,* November 4, 1941

"Doggonit," said the second boy. "I hope them birds got poison in they feet!"

The two small boys, Riley and Buster, sat on the floor of the porch, their bare feet resting upon the cool earth as they stared past the line on the paving where the sun consumed the shade, to a yard directly across the street. The grass in the yard was very green, and a house stood against it, neat and white in the morning sun. A double row of trees stood alongside the house, heavy with cherries that showed deep red against the dark green of the leaves and dull dark brown of the branches. The two boys were watching an old man who rocked himself in a chair as he stared back at them across the street.

"Just look at him," said Buster. "Ole Rogan's so scared we gonna git some a his ole cherries he ain't even got sense enough to go in outa the sun!"

"Well, them birds is gitting their'n," said Riley.

"They mockingbirds."

"I don't care what kinda birds they is, they sho in them trees."

"Yeah, ole Rogan don't see *them.* Man, I tell you white folks ain't got no sense."

They were silent now, watching the darting flight of the birds into the trees. Behind them they could hear the clatter of a sewing machine: Riley's mother was sewing for the white folks. It was quiet, and as the woman worked, her voice rose above the whirring machine in song.

"Your mama sho can sing, man," said Buster.

"She sings in the choir," said Riley, "and she sings all the leads in church."

"Shucks, I know it," said Buster. "You tryin' to brag?"

As they listened they heard the voice rise clear and liquid to float upon the morning air:

"I got wings, you got wings,
All God's chillun got a wings
When I git to heaven gonna put on my wings
Gonna shout all ovah God's heab'n.
Heab'n, heab'n
Everbody talkin' 'bout heab'n ain't going there
Heab'n, heab'n, Ah'm gonna fly all ovah God's heab'n . . ."

She sang as though the words possessed a deep and throbbing meaning for her, and the boys stared blankly at the earth, feeling the somber, mysterious calm of church. The street was quiet, and even old Rogan had stopped rocking to listen. Finally the voice trailed off to a hum and became lost in the clatter of the busy machine.

"Wish I could sing like that," said Buster.

Riley was silent, looking down to the end of the porch where the sun had eaten a bright square into the shade, fixing a flitting butterfly in its brilliance.

"What would you do if you had wings?" he said.

"Shucks, I'd outfly an eagle. I wouldn't stop flying till I was a million, billion, trillion, zillion miles away from this ole town."

"Where'd you go, man?"

"Up north, maybe to Chicago."

"Man, if I had wings I wouldn't never settle down."

"Me neither. Hecks, with wings you could go anywhere, even up to the sun if it wasn't too hot . . ."

". . . I'd go to New York . . ."

"Even around the stars . . ."

"Or Dee-troit, Michigan . . ."

"Hell, you could git some cheese off the moon and some milk from the Milky Way . . ."

"Or anywhere else colored is free . . ."

"I bet I'd loop-the-loop . . ."

"And parachute . . ."

"I'd land in Africa and git me some diamonds . . ."

"Yeah, and them cannibals would eat the hell outa you, too," said Riley.

"The heck they would, not fast as I'd fly away . . ."

"Man, they'd catch you and stick some them long spears in your behin'!" said Riley.

Buster laughed as Riley shook his head gravely: "Boy, you'd look like a black pincushion when they got through with you," said Riley.

"Shucks, man, they couldn't catch me, them suckers is too lazy. The geography book says they 'bout the most lazy folks in the whole world," said Buster with disgust, "just black and lazy!"

"Aw naw, they ain't neither," exploded Riley.

"They is too! The geography book says they is!"

"Well, my ole man says they ain't!"

"How come they ain't then?"

" 'Cause my old man says that over there they got kings and diamonds and gold and ivory, and if they got all them things, all of 'em caint be lazy," said Riley. "Ain't many colored folks over here got them things."

"Sho ain't, man. The white folks won't let 'em," said Buster.

It was good to think that all the Africans were not lazy. He tried to remember all he had heard of Africa as he watched a purple pigeon sail down into the street and scratch where a horse had passed. Then, as he remembered a story his teacher had told him, he saw a car rolling swiftly up the street and the pigeon stretching its wings and lifting easily into the air, skimming the top of the car in its slow, rocking flight. He watched it rise and disappear where the taut telephone wires cut the sky above the curb. Buster felt good. Riley scratched his initials in the soft earth with his big toe.

"Riley, you know all them Africa guys ain't really that lazy," he said.

"I know they ain't," said Riley. "I just tole you so."

"Yeah, but my teacher tole me, too. She tole us 'bout one of the African guys named Toussan what she said whipped Napoleon!"

Riley stopped scratching in the earth and looked up, his eye rolling in disgust: "Now how come you have to start lying?"

"Thass what she said."

"Boy, you oughta quit telling them things."

"I hope God may kill me."

"She said he was a *African?*"

"Cross my heart, man . . ."

"Really?"

"Really, man. She said he come from a place named Hayti."

Riley looked hard at Buster and, seeing the seriousness of the face, felt the excitement of a story rise up within him.

"Buster, I'll bet a fat man you lyin'. What'd that teacher say?"

"Really, man, she said that Toussan and his men got up

on one of them African mountains and shot down them peckerwood soldiers fass as they'd try to come up . . ."

"Why good-God-a-mighty!" yelled Riley.

"Oh boy, they shot 'em down!" chanted Buster.

"Tell me about it, man!"

"And they throwed 'em off the mountain . . ."

". . . Goool-leee! . . ."

". . . And Toussan drove 'em cross the sand . . ."

". . . Yeah! And what was they wearing, Buster? . . ."

"Man, they had on red uniforms and blue hats all trimmed with gold and they had some swords all shining, what they called sweet blades of Damascus . . ."

"Sweet blades of Damascus! . . ."

". . . They really had 'em," chanted Buster.

"And what kinda guns?"

"Big, black cannon!"

"And where did ole what you call 'im run them guys? . . ."

"His name was Toussan."

"Toozan! Just like Tarzan . . ."

"Not Taar-zan, dummy, Toou-zan!"

"Toussan! And where'd ole Toussan run 'em?"

"Down to the water, man . . ."

". . . To the river water . . ."

". . . Where some great big ole boats was waiting for 'em . . ."

". . . Go on, Buster!"

"An' Toussan shot into them boats . . ."

". . . He shot into 'em . . ."

". . . shot into them boats . . ."

"Jesus! . . ."

". . . with his great big cannons . . ."

". . . Yeah! . . ."

". . . made a-brass . . ."

". . . Brass . . ."

". . . an' his big black cannonballs started killin' them peckerwoods . . ."

". . . Lawd, Lawd . . ."

". . . Boy, till them peckerwoods hollowed, *Please, Please, Mister Toussan, we'll be good!*"

"An' what'd Toussan tell 'em, Buster?"

"Boy, he said in his deep voice, *I oughta drown all a you bastards.*"

"An' what'd the peckerwoods say?"

"They said, *Please, Please, Please, Mister Toussan . . .*"

". . . We'll be good," broke in Riley.

"Thass right, man," said Buster excitedly. He clapped his hands and kicked his heels against the earth, his black face glowing in a burst of rhythmic joy.

"Boy!"

"And what'd ole Toussan say then?"

"He said in his big deep voice: *You all peckerwoods better be good, 'cause this is sweet Papa Toussan talking and my nigguhs is crazy 'bout white meat!*"

"Ho, ho, ho!" Riley bent double with laughter. The rhythm still throbbed within him and he wanted the story to go on and on . . .

"Buster, you know didn't no teacher tell you that lie," he said.

"Yes she did, man."

"She said there was really a guy like that what called himself Sweet Papa Toussan?"

Riley's voice was unbelieving, and there was a wistful expression in his eyes that Buster could not understand. Finally he dropped his head and grinned.

"Well," he said, "I bet thass what ole Toussan said. You know how grown folks is, they caint tell a story right 'cepting real old folks like Granma."

"They sho caint," said Riley. "They don't know how to put the right stuff to it."

Riley stood, his legs spread wide, and stuck his thumbs in the top of his trousers, swaggering sinisterly.

"Come on, watch me do it now, Buster. Now I bet ole Toussan looked down at them white folks standing just about like this and said in a soft easy voice: *Ain't I done begged you white folks to quit messin' with me?* . . ."

"Thass right, quit messing with 'im," chanted Buster.

"But naw, you all had to come on anyway . . ."

". . . Just 'cause they was black . . ."

"Thass right," said Riley. "Then ole Toussan felt so damn bad and mad the tears came a-trickling down . . ."

". . . He was really mad."

"And then, man, he said in his big, bad voice: *Goddamn you white folks, how come you all caint let us colored alone?*"

". . . An' he was crying . . ."

". . . An' Toussan tole them peckerwoods: *I been beggin' you all to quit bothering us* . . ."

". . . Beggin' on his bended knees! . . ."

"Then, man, Toussan got real mad and snatched off his hat and started stompin' up and down on it and the tears was tricklin' down and he said: *You all come tellin' me about Napoleon* . . ."

"They was tryin' to scare 'im, man . . ."

"Said: *I don't give a damn about Napoleon* . . ."

". . . Wasn't studyin' 'bout him . . ."

". . . Toussan said: *Napoleon ain't nothing but a man!* Then Toussan pulled back his shining sword like this, and twirled it at them peckerwoods' throats so hard it z-z-z-zinged in the air!"

"Now keep on, finish it, man," said Buster. "What'd Toussan do then?"

"Then you know what he did, he said: *I oughta beat the hell outa you peckerwoods!*"

"Thass right, and he did it too," said Buster. He jumped to his feet and fenced violently with five desperate imaginary soldiers, running each through with his imaginary sword. Buster watched him from the porch, grinning.

"Toussan musta scared them white folks almost to death!"

"Yeah, thass 'bout the way it was," said Buster. The rhythm was dying now and he sat back upon the porch, breathing tiredly.

"It sho is a good story," said Riley.

"Hecks, man, all the stories my teacher tells us is good. She's a good ole teacher—but you know one thing?"

"Naw, what?"

"Ain't none of them stories in the books. Wonder why?"

"Hell, you know why, Ole Toussan was too hard on them white folks, thass why."

"Oh, he was a hard man!"

"He was mean . . ."

"But a good mean!"

"Toussan was clean . . ."

". . . He was a good, clean mean," said Riley.

"Aw, man, he was sooo-preme," said Buster.

"Riiiley!!"

The boys stopped short in their word play, their mouths wide.

"Riley, I say!" It was Riley's mother's voice.

"Ma'm?"

"She musta heard us cussin'," whispered Buster.

"Shut up, man . . . What you want, Ma?"

"I says I want you all to go round the backyard and play. You keeping up too much fuss out there. White folks says we tear up a neighborhood when we move in it and you all out there jus provin' them out true. Now git on round in the back."

"Aw, Ma, we was jus playing, Ma . . ."

"Boy, I said for you all to go on."

"But, Ma . . ."

"You hear me, boy!"

"Yessum, we going," said Riley. "Come on, Buster."

Buster followed slowly behind, feeling the dew upon his feet as he walked up on the shaded grass.

"What else did he do, man?" Buster said.

"Huh? Rogan?"

"Hecks, naw! I'm talkin' 'bout Toussan."

"Doggone if I know, man—but I'm gonna ask that teacher."

"He was a fightin' son-of-a-gun, wasn't he, man?"

"He didn't stand for no foolishness," said Riley reservedly. He thought of other things now, and as he moved along, he slid his feet easily over the short-cut grass, dancing as he chanted:

Iron is iron,
And tin is tin,

And that's the way
The story . . .

"Aw come on, man," interrupted Buster. "Let's go play in the alley . . ."

And that's the way . . .

"Maybe we can slip around and get some cherries," Buster went on.

. . . the story ends, chanted Riley.

Afternoon

The two boys stood at the rear of a vacant lot looking up at a telephone pole. The wires strung from one pole to the next gleamed bright copper in the summer sun. Glints of green light shot from the pole's glass insulators as the boys stared.

"Funny ain't no birds on them wires, huh?"

"They got too much 'lectricity in 'em. You can even hear 'em hum they got so much."

Riley cocked his head, listening:

"That what's making that noise?" he said.

"Sho, man. Jus like if you put your ear against a street-

From *American Writing,* 1940

car-line pole you can tell when the car's coming. You don't even have to see it," Buster said.

"Thass right, I knowed about that."

"Wonder why they have them glass things up there?"

"To keep them guys what climbs up there from gitting shocked, I guess."

Riley caught the creosote smell of the black paint on the pole as his eyes traveled over its rough surface.

"High as a bitch!" he said.

"It ain't so high I bet I caint hit that glass on the end there."

"Buster, you fulla brown. You caint hit *that* glass, it's too high."

"Shucks!! Gimme a rock."

They looked slowly over the dry ground for a rock.

"Here's a good one," Riley called. "An egg rock."

"Throw it here, and watch how ole Lou Gehrig snags 'em on first base."

Riley pitched. The rock came high and swift. Buster stretched his arm to catch it and kicked out his right leg behind him, touching base.

"And he's out on first!" he cried.

"You got 'im all right," Riley said.

"You jus watch this."

Riley watched as Buster wound up his arm and pointed to the insulator with his left hand. His body gave a twist and the rock flew upward.

Crack!

Pieces of green glass sprinkled down.

They stood with hands on hips, looking about them. A bird twittered. A rooster crowed. No one shouted to them and they laughed nervously.

"What'd I tell you?"

"Damn! I never thought you could do it."

"We better get away from here in case somebody saw that."

Riley looked around: "Come on."

They walked out to the alley.

Chickens crouched in the cool earth beneath a shade tree. The two boys hurried out of sight of a woman piling rubbish in the next yard. A row of fence stretched up the alley, past garages and outhouses. They walked carefully, avoiding burrs and pieces of glass, over ground hot to their bare feet. The alley smelled of dust and the dry pungence of burning leaves.

Buster picked up a stick and stirred in the weeds behind an unpainted garage. It raised dust, causing him to sneeze.

"Buster, what the hell you doing?"

"Looking for liquor, man."

"Looking for *liquor*?"

"Sho, man." He stopped, pointing: "See that house down on the corner?"

Riley saw the back of a small green house with a row of zinc tubs on the rail of its porch.

"Yeah, I see it," he said.

"Bootleggers live down there. They hid it all along here in these weeds. Boy, one night the cops raided and they was carrying it outa there in slop jars and everything."

"In *slop* jars?"

"Hell yes!"

"Gee, the cops catch 'em?"

"Hell naw, they poured it all down the toilet. Man, I bet all the fish in the Canadian River was drunk."

They laughed noisily.

Buster dug in the weeds again, then stopped:

"Guess ain't nothing in here."

He looked at Riley. Riley was grinning to himself.

"Boy, what's the matter with you?"

"Buster, I'm still thinking about 'em throwing that liquor down the toilet. You know one thing? When I was little and they would set me on the seat, I useta think the devil was down there gitting him some cigars. I was scaired to sit down. Man, one time my ole lady like to beat the hell outa me 'cause I wouldn't sit down."

"You crazy, man," Buster said. "Didn't I tell you, you was crazy?"

"Honest," Riley said. "I useta believe that."

They laughed. Buster dragged his stick through the weed tops. A hen cackled in the yard beyond the fence they were moving past. The sound of someone practicing scales on a piano drifted to them. They walked slowly.

The narrow road through the alley was cut with dried ruts of wagon wheels, the center embedded with pieces of broken glass. "Where we going?" Buster asked. Riley began to chant:

"Well I met Mister Rabbit
down by the pea vine . . ."

Buster joined in:

"An' I asked him where's he gwine
Well, he said, Just kiss my behind
And he skipped on down the pea vine."

Buster suddenly stopped and grabbed his nose.

"Look at that ole dead cat!"

"Ain't on my mama's table."

"Mine neither!"

"You better spit on it, else you'll have it for supper," Buster said.

They spat upon the maggot-ridden body, and moved on.

"Always lots a dead cats in the alley. Wonder why?"

"Dogs get 'em, I guess."

"My dog ate so many dead cats once, he went crazy and died," said Riley.

"I don't like cats. They too sly."

"Sho stinks!"

"I'm holding my breath."

"Me too!"

Soon they passed the smell. Buster stopped, pointing.

"Look at the apples on that tree."

"Gittin' big as hell!"

"Sho is, let's git some."

"Naw, they'll give you the flux. They too green."

"I'm taking a chance," Buster said.

"Think anybody's home?"

"Hell, we don't have to go inside the fence. See, some of 'em's hanging over the alley."

They walked over to the fence and looked into the yard. The earth beneath the trees was bare and moist. Up near the house the grass was short and neat. Flagstones leading out of the garage made a pattern in the grass.

"White folks live here?"

"Naw, colored. White folks moved out when we moved in the block," Buster said.

They looked up into the tree: the sun broke through the leaves and apples hung bright green from dull black branches. A snake-doctor hummed by in long, curving flight. It was quiet and they could hear the thump, thump, thump of oil wells pumping away to the south. Buster stepped back from the fence, and held his stick ready.

"Look out now," Buster said. "They might fall in the weeds."

The stick ripped the leaves. An apple rattled through the branches, thumping to the ground inside the fence.

"Damn!"

He picked up the stick and threw again. The leaves rustled; Riley caught an apple. Another fell near Buster's toes. He looked at Riley's apple.

"I git the biggest! You scaired to eat 'em anyway."

Riley watched him an instant, rolling the apple between his palms. There was a spot of red on the green of the apple.

"I don't care," he said finally. "You can have it."

He pitched the apple to Buster. Buster caught it and touched first base with his toe.

"He's out on first!"

"Let's go," Riley said.

They walked close to the fence, the weeds whipping their thin legs. A woodpecker drummed on a telephone pole.

"I'm gonna remember that tree. Won't be long before them apples is ripe."

"Yeah, but this *here'n* sho ain't ripe," Riley said. Buster laughed as he saw Riley's face twist into a wry frown.

"We need some salt," he said.

"Man, damn! Hot springs water won't help this apple none."

Buster laughed and batted a tin can against a fence with his stick. A dog growled and sniffed on the other side. Buster growled back and the dog went barking along the fence as they moved past.

"Sic 'im, Rin Tin Tin, sic 'im," Riley called.

Buster barked. They went past the fence, the dog still barking behind them.

Buster dropped his stick and fitted his apple carefully into his fingers. Riley watched him.

"See, here's the way you hold it to pitch a curve," Buster said.

"How?"

"Like this: these two fingers this here way; you put your thumb this here way, and you let it roll off your fingers this a way."

Riley gripped his apple as Buster showed him; then wound up and threw. The apple flew up the alley in a straight line and suddenly broke sharply to the right.

"See there! You see it break? That's the way you do it, man. You put that one right up around the batter's neck."

Riley was surprised. A grin broke over his face and his eyes fell upon Buster with admiration. Buster ran and picked up the apple.

"See, here's the way you do it."

He wound up and pitched, the apple humming as it whipped through the air. Riley saw it coming at him and curving suddenly, sharply away. It fell behind him. He shook his head, smiling:

"Buster?"

"What?"

"Boy, you 'bout the throwin'est nigguh I ever seen. Less

see you hit that post yonder, that one over there by the fence."

"Hell, man! You must think I'm Schoolboy Rowe or somebody."

"Go on, Buster, you can hit it."

Buster took a bite out of the apple and chewed as he wound up his arm. Then suddenly he bent double and snapped erect, his left foot leaving the ground and his right arm whipping forward.

Clunk!

The apple smashed against the post and burst into flying pieces.

"What'd I tell you? Damn, that ole apple come apart like when you hit a quail solid with a shotgun."

"Thass what you call control," Buster said.

"I don't know what you call it, but I'd sho hate to have you throwin' bricks at me," said Riley.

"Shucks, you ain't seen nothin'. You want to see some throwin' you jus wait till we pass through the fairgrounds to go swimming in Goggleye Lake. Man, the nigguhs out there can throw Coca-Cola bottles so hard that they bust in the air!"

Riley doubled himself up, laughing.

"Buster, you better quit lying so much!"

"I ain't lying, man. You can ask anybody."

"Boy, boy!" Riley laughed. The saliva bubbled at the corners of his mouth.

"Come on over to my house and sit in the cool," Buster said.

They turned a corner and walked into a short stretch of grassy yard before a gray cottage. A breeze blew across the porch; it smelled clean and fresh to Riley. The wooden boards of the porch had been washed white. Buster remembered seeing his mother scrubbing the porch with the suds after she had finished the clothes. He tried to forget those clothes.

A fly buzzed at the door screen. Riley dropped down on the porch, his bare feet dangling.

"Wait a minute while I see what's here to eat," Buster said.

Riley lay back and covered his eyes with his arm. "All right," he said.

Buster went inside, fanning flies away from the door. He could hear his mother busy in the kitchen as he walked through the little house. She was standing before the window, ironing. When he stepped down into the kitchen she turned her head.

"Buster, where you been, you lazy rascal! You knowed I wanted you here to help me with them tubs!"

"I was over to Riley's, Ma. I didn't know you wanted me."

"You didn't know! Lawd, I don't know why I had to have a chile like you. I work my fingers to the bone to keep you looking decent and that's the way you 'preciates it. You didn't know!"

Buster was silent. It was always this way. He had meant to help; he always meant to do the right thing, but something always got in the way.

"Well what you standing there looking like a dying calf for? I'm through now. Go on out and play."

"Yessum."

He turned and walked slowly out of the back door.

The cat arched its back against his leg as he went off the

porch, stepping gingerly over the sun-heated boards. The ground around the steps was still moist and white where Ma had poured the suds. A stream of water trickled rapidly from the hydrant, sparkling silver in the sunlight. Suddenly he remembered why he had gone into the house. He stopped and called:

"Maaa . . ."

"What you want?"

"Ma, what we gonna have for supper?"

"Lawd, all you think about is your gut. I don't know. Come on back in here and fix you some eggs if you hongery. I'm too busy to stop—and for the Lawd's sake leave me alone!"

Buster hesitated. He was hungry but he could not stay around Ma when she was like this. She was like this whenever something went wrong with her and the white folks. Her voice had been like a slap in the face. He started slowly around to the front of the house. The dust was thick and warm to his feet. Looking down, he broke a sprig of milkweed between his bare toes and watched the green stem slowly bleeding white sap upon the brown earth. A tiny globe of milk glistened on his toe, and as he walked to the front of the house he dug his foot into the dry dust, leaving the sap a small spot of mud.

He dropped down beside Riley.

"You eat so quick?" asked Riley.

"Naw, Ma's mad at me."

"Don't pay that no mind, man. My folks is always after me. They think all a man wants to do is what they want him to. You oughta be glad you ain't go no ole man like I got."

"Is he very mean?"

"My ole man's so mean he hates hisself!"

"Ma's bad enough. Let them white folks make her mad where she works and I catch hell."

"My ole man's the same way. Boy, and can he beat you! One night he come home from work and was gonna beat my ass with a piece of 'lectricity wire. But my ole lady stopped 'im. Told 'im he bet' not."

"Wonder why they so mean," Buster said.

"Damn if I know. My ole man says we don't git enough beatings these days. He said Gramma useta tie 'em up in a gunny sack and smoke 'em, like they do hams. He was gonna do that to me. But Ma stopped 'im. She said, 'Don't you come treating no chile of mine like no slave. Your Ma mighta raised you like a slave, but I ain't raising him like that and you bet' not harm a hair of his head!' And he didn't do it neither. Man, was I glad!"

"Damn! I'm glad I don't have no ole man," Buster said.

"You just wait till I get big. Boy, I'm gonna beat the hell outa my ole man. I'm gonna learn to box like Jack Johnson, just so I can beat his ass."

"Jack Johnson, first colored heavyweight champion of the whole wide world!" Buster said. "Wonder where he is now?"

"I don't know, up north in New York, I guess. But I bet *wherever* he is, ain't nobody messing with him."

"You mighty right! I heard my Uncle Luke say Jack Johnson was a better fighter than Joe Louis. Said he was fast as a cat on his feet. Fast as a cat! Gee, you can throw a cat off the top a house and he'll land on his feet. Why by golly, I bet you could throw a cat down from heaven and the son-of-a-bitch would land right side up!"

"My ole man's always singing:

'If it hadn't a been
for the referee
Jack Johnson woulda killed
Jim Jefferie,' "

Riley said.

The afternoon was growing old. The sun hung low in a cloudless sky and soon would be lost behind the fringe of trees across the street. A faint wind blew and the leaves on the trees trembled in the sun. They were silent now. A black-and-yellow wasp flew beneath the eaves, droning. Buster watched it disappear inside its gray honeycomblike nest, then rested back on his elbows and crossed his legs, thinking of Jack Johnson. A screen slammed loudly somewhere down the street. Riley lay beside him, whistling a tune between his teeth.

That I Had the Wings

Riley stared into the peach tree, his eyes wide with excitement. Right there, straight up where the pink blossoms had burst the sticky buds, a mama robin redbreast was teaching a little robin how to fly. First the mama bird would fly a piece and chirp to the young bird to follow her. But the little bird wouldn't move. Then the mama bird would fly back and peck the young one and circle around and try to push it off the branch and the little bird held on, afraid.

Shoots, why don't yuh go on an' try it, thought Riley. Go on, li'l bird. Don't be scaired. But the little robin just sat there fanning its wings and cheeping. Then Riley saw the

From *Common Ground,* Summer 1943

old robin fly off into a nearby tree. See there, she done gone an' got mad with yuh, he thought. Shoots, I bet I could make yuh fly. He started to lie back on the porch beside Buster, when suddenly he saw the young robin flutter its ragged wings and leap. His breath tensed. The bird struggled in the air, fluttering, falling, down; beating its wings wildly against the earth. He started up. But there it was, trying to rise and fly awkwardly, up to where the mama bird chattered in the tree.

Riley sat back. He felt good. "Yuh had me fooled," he whispered to the young robin. "Yuh wuzn't really scaired. Yuh jus didn't want no ole folks messin' with yuh." He felt very good. Suddenly he tensed. I'm gon git me a bird an' teach him how to fly, he decided. Then as he turned to wake Buster and tell him, Buster stirred and opened his eyes.

"Man, les do something," said Buster in his husky voice. "How come yuh caint go nowhere?"

Riley's spirits sagged. He had forgotten. "Aw, 'cause somebody tole about us gittin' after them bad-luck church house squabs, and Ma tole Aunt Kate to keep me in the yard."

"Hecks, them pigeons don't belong to the church," said Buster. "They jus lives there. Don't nobody own 'em. I wish I had me some a that good ole flyin' meat right now!"

Riley looked for the robin, seeing it flutter into a distant tree, and was filled with a strange loneliness. If I didn't have to stay here, he thought, we could go find us a bird.

Buster stood. "I guess I be seein' yuh, man. I feels like doin' somethin'."

"Aw, don't go," pleaded Riley. "We kin fin' somethin' to do. . . . Say!" he challenged with sudden inspiration. "I bet yuh don't know this verse!"

"Which'un?"

"This'un:

"If I was the president
Of these United States
Said if I was the president
Of these United States
I'd eat good chocolate candy bars
An' swing on the White House gates—
Great—God-a-mighty, man—
I'd swing on them White House gates!"

"Yuh Riiley!!!"

His mouth fell open. Aunt Kate stood in the shadow of the doorway, her wrinkled face quivering with rage.

"Ah heahed yuh, suh! Ah heahed yuh takin' the Lawd's name in vain!"

He scrambled to his feet, speechless.

"An' yuh wuz talkin' 'bout bein' the president! Yuh know yo ma's done taught yuh better'n that! Yuh better min', suh, befo yuh git everybody into trouble. What yuh think would happen to yo po ma if the white folks wuz to hear she wuz raisin' up a black chile whut's got no better sense than to talk 'bout bein' president?"

"It wuz jus a verse," stammered Riley. "I didn't mean no harm."

"Yass, but it wuz a *sinful* verse! The Lawd don't like it an' the white folks wouldn't neither."

Catching a glimpse of the young robin flying into a farther tree, he made himself look meek. "I'm sorry, Aunt Kate."

Her face softened. "Yuh chillun havta learn how to live

right while yuh young, so's yuh kin have some peace when yuh gits grown. Else yuh be buttin' yo head 'ginst a col' white wall all yo born days. Ahm ole as Ah is today jus 'cause Ah didn't let them kinda sinful thoughts worry ma min'." She pursed her lips in proud conviction.

Riley looked at her from under lowered lids. It was always God, or the white folks. She always made him feel guilty, as though he had done something wrong he could never remember, for which he would never be forgiven. Like when white folks stared at you on the street. Suddenly Aunt Kate's face changed from dark anger to intense sweetness, making him wary and confused.

"Yuh chillun needs to learn some a the Lawd's songs," she beamed, singing:

"Sing aaa-ho that
Ah had the wings of-vah dove
Ah'd fly to mah Jesus an'
Be at res' . . ."

"Thass the kinda song fo yuh chillun to sing. Yuh needs the wings of the spirit to help yuh through this worl'. Lemme heah yuh try it erlong with me."

"Sing aaa-ho that—,"

Riley's throat was dry. The little robin was winging itself out of sight now. He looked helplessly at Buster. Buster looked away. Aunt Kate paused, her face clouding.

"I-I-I guess I don't feel . . . like . . . singin' jus now, Aunt Kate," he said fearfully.

"So now yuh don't feel like it!" she exploded. "If I wuz

teachin' yuh some a that devil's trash yuh wuz singin', yuh'd feel like it though!"

"B-b-but it wuzn't no bad song."

"Hush that 'sputin' mah word! Ah kin see that the devil's gon git yuh, suh! Jus git on to the back an' outa mah sight!"

He started slowly.

"Git, suh! Yuh nasty stinkin' imp-a-satan! Yuh jus mark mah word. Befo the day's gone, yuh gon git into some sorta trouble an Ahm gon have yo ma beat the fear a God into yuh!"

He went, stepping slowly off the porch, and entered the shadow between the two houses.

"I'd sho hate to have her put her mouth on me like that," whispered Buster. "Man, they say ole folks like that kin put a terrible jinx on yuh!"

Riley leaned against the house. That wuzn't no bad verse; it was a funny one. He'd put in the "great-God-a-mighty" part himself, to make it sound better. Shucks! Aunt Kate sho wuz a puzzle—maybe she wuz too ole to understand a man—born way back in slavery times. All she knows is go to church every night and read the Bible and mess with him while Ma was working for the white folks during the day. She's crazy. That ole song: *Sing a-ho if I had the wings of a dove* . . . Ain't no fun singin' that ole song.

Suddenly a grin bloomed on his face.

"Hey, Buster," he whispered.

"Whut?"

He sang huskily:

"If I had the wings of a dove, Aunt Kate,
I'd eat up all the candy, Lawd,
An' tear down the White House gate. . . ."

Buster stuck out his lower lip and frowned. "Fool, yuh better stop that makin' fun a that church song. Aunt Kate said it was a sin."

Riley's laughter wavered. Maybe God would punish him. He bit his lip. But the words kept dancing in his mind. Lots of verses. *Amazin' grace, how sweet the sound. A bullfrog slapped his granma down.* He felt the suppressed laughter clicking and rolling within him, like big blue marbles. That "amazin' grace" part was from a church song too. Maybe he would really be punished now. But he could suppress it no longer and leaned against the house and laughed.

"Yuh jus keep on laughin' at that church song an' I'm gonna go fin' me some other guys to play with," warned Buster.

"Aw, I wuzn't laughin' at that," he lied.

"Then whut wuz yuh laughin' at?"

" 'Bout . . . 'bout yesterday when I fell off the church house . . ."

"When we wuz after that flyin' meat?"

"Yeah."

"Fool, that wuzn't funny. Yuh wuz cryin' up a breeze. Ain't yo head still sore?"

He felt his head. "Just a little," he said.

"I bet yuh was really scaired," said Buster.

"The heck I wuz. I felt pretty good."

"Boy, yuh quit that lyin', yuh wuz cryin' like a baby!"

"Shucks, I'm talkin' 'bout *when* I wuz fallin'. I cried 'cause I hit my head."

"Yuh jus tryin' to fool me," said Buster. "Yuh like to busted yo brains out."

"Hones', man. Thass how come them white guys like to jump outa them airplanes in them parachutes."

"Yeah, but yuh didn't have no parachute," laughed Buster.

Riley walked toward where a shaft of sunlight broke the shadow at the back of the house. "Man, yuh don't know nothin'," he said. "Les go look at the new baby chicks."

They came to the chicken fence and swayed gently against it, looking through. Bits of grain and droppings were scattered about, and the hard earth was marked with strange designs where the chickens had scratched. The chickens eyed them expectantly.

Riley pointed to a brood of downy baby chicks scurrying about an old white hen.

"There's the li'l biddies," he cried. "They cute, ain't they, man?"

"They sho is!" Buster's eyes gleamed with pleasure.

"An lissen to all that fuss them li'l guys is makin'."

"Shucks, man, they cryin'. Most ever'thin whut's little cries, like my baby brother, Bubber."

"Ma cries when she's in church," said Riley, "an' she ain't little."

"Aw, thass when she's shoutin', man."

"I don't like nothin' like that," said Riley. "How come they have to shout?"

"'Cause they feels the *spirit*. Thass why."

"Well, what's the spirit?"

"Fool, thass the Holy Ghost! Yuh been to Sunday school."

Riley wiggled his toes through the wire.

"Well, all I know is the Holy Ghost sho mus hurt bad, 'cause eve'body gits to cryin' and cuttin' the fool," he said finally.

"Ma says when they cries is when they feelin' good," said Buster.

"Well, feelin' good or no feelin' good, when I see Ma cryin' an' goin' on like that I feel so shame I could hide my face," he said tightly. "I don't like nothin' yuh have to cry over befo yuh kin feel good."

He saw two young cockerels plunging headlong across the yard, flapping their stubby wings and squawking.

"Chickens is crazy!" cried Buster. "Jus look at them two fool roosters goin' yonder!"

Riley dismissed them with a scornful wave of his palm. "Them ain't no roosters, man. There's a *real* rooster over yonder," he said, pointing.

"Good-God-a-mighty! That mus be the boss rooster!"

"He is. Name's Ole Bill."

"Ole Bill!"

"Man, an' he can whip anything whut wears feathers," bragged Riley.

Buster whistled in admiration. The silky sheen of the rooster's red and dark green plumage rippled in the sun. Ole Bill clucked to the hens and strutted, his red comb swaying in proud dignity.

"Jus look at that fool," exclaimed Buster, "liftin' his feet up and down like a big fat preacher."

"An' look at his spurs," cried Riley. "Look at his spurs!"

"Doggone! Them hens better watch that fool!"

"He can fight with 'em too, man. When he gits them spurs into another chicken, he jus rides right on to the promise' lan'."

Ole Bill clucked softly and the hens scurried to where he scratched.

"Man, man! He's the fightin'est, crowin'est rooster in the whole wide world!"

Suddenly the rooster flapped his wings and crowed, his chest swelling and his neck arching forward with the sound.

"Lissen to that son-of-a-gun!"

"Aaaaw, sing it, Bill!"

"Man, thass li'l Gabriel!"

"Shucks, he's the Louie Armstrong of the chickens!"

"Blowin his golden trumpet, Lawd . . ."

"An' tellin' all the roosters they better be good . . ."

" 'Cause he won't stan for no foolishness . . ."

"Ole Bill says, *Tell all the dogs, an' tell all the cats, they better be good or go join the bats,*" rhymed Riley, " *'cause the mighty Ole Bill's in town.*"

"Naw, naw, man. He's the Louie Armstrong of the chickens playing 'Hold That Tiger . . .' "

"Yeah, tellin' that tiger not to act no fool . . ."

"Thass it, hittin' high *p* . . ."

"Boy, ain't no *p* on no horn. It's *do re me,*" sang Riley.

"Yeah, 'tis. When Louie plays it, 'tis. It's *do re me fa sol la ti* an' *p* too!"

They bent double with laughter. Ole Bill arched his neck and swallowed, his sharp bill parting like the curved blades of a pair of scissors.

Riley became sober. "My ole man is really proud of that there rooster," he said. "If yuh want to make him mad, jus tell him Ole Bill got run over. Corse, I don't blame him, 'cause if I wuz to die and come back a bird like Aunt Kate says folks do, I'd want to be just like Ole Bill."

"Not me," said Buster. "I wouldn't want to come back no rooster."

"How come? Ole Bill's good-lookin' an' he can fight like Joe Louis!"

"Shucks, but he caint fly!"

"The heck he caint fly!"

"Caint *no* roosters fly!"

"I kin prove it!"

"Yuh crazy, Riley. How yuh gon prove a rooster kin fly?"

"Easy. I'll git up on top of the chicken house and yuh han' Ole Bill up to me—"

"Aw naw," said Buster. "Aw naw. I ain't goin' in there with all them spurs."

Riley spat in disgust. "Yuh make me sick."

"Yeah? Well I still ain't goin' in there."

"Awright, yuh go on top an' I'll han' him up to yuh. Okay?"

"Okay. I don't guess he kin spur me when he's off the ground."

Riley glanced furtively toward where Aunt Kate usually sat at the kitchen window, then entered the yard, fastening the gate behind him.

"Hurry up, man," called Buster from the roof. "It's hot up here."

"Gimme time," called Riley. "Jus gimme time."

He moved stealthily toward Ole Bill, brushing along the fence. The hens squawked. Ole Bill stepped angrily about, his head jerking rapidly.

"Yuh better watch that fool," yelled Buster.

"Who yuh tellin'? *Come here to me, Ole Bill!*"

As he reached out, the big rooster charged, his neck feathers standing out like a ruff, his legs churning the air, spurring. Riley covered his face with his arm.

"Grab holt to him, man!"

He lunged, grabbing. The dust flew. Ole Bill struck the ground and danced away. Riley dived, seeing Ole Bill bounce away like a puffed-up feather duster.

"What I tell yuh 'bout this fool?" he panted.

"Yuh sho didn't tell no lie. *Watch 'im!*"

The charge took Riley unaware. He went over fast, landing hard. He couldn't breathe. The rooster swarmed over him. He guarded his eyes. The rooster clawed his legs, pecked at his face. He felt a spur go into his shirt, the point against his ribs. Little evil yellow eyes, old like Aunt Kate's, danced sinisterly over his face. As his hand connected with a horny leg, he heard his shirt rip and held on, the pungent odor of dusty feathers hot in his nostrils. Panting, he scrambled to his feet. Ole Bill jerked powerfully, the scaly legs rough to his hands, the sharp bill stabbing.

"Hold 'im till I git down there!" yelled Buster.

"Hecks, I almost got him now," he panted. He held the rooster over his head, trying to keep his face clear of the whipping wings. Suddenly he pinned the wings to Ole Bill's sides and gave a heave, his body arching backward, sending the rooster sailing across the yard. The air filled with dust as Ole Bill skidded. Riley whirled, sneezing and running for the gate, then stopped. The rooster was shaking the dust from his feathers. Watching him out of the corner of his eye, Riley walked slowly, deliberately, so that Buster would not think he was afraid. Before him the old hen was herding her brood out of his path. Obeying a sudden impulse, he swooped up two of the chicks and stepped swiftly outside the gate.

"Fool, yuh better come on outa there," warned Buster.

"I ain't scaired like yuh," he taunted. But it was a relief to be outside.

"Take these," he called as he started to climb up to the roof.

"Whut?"

"Aw, take 'em, fraidy. These li'l ones won't spur yuh."

Buster reached down and cradled the yellow chicks in his short brown fingers.

Riley leaped up, catching the slanting roof. A line of brown ants hurried nervously down the gray sunheated boards. He hoisted himself carefully, placing his hands and knees so as not to crush the ants. Up on top, he took the peeping chicks and placed them carefully inside his torn shirt. They were soft, like bolls of cotton.

"Yuh liable to smother 'em, man," said Buster.

"Naw, I won't. See, they ain't even cryin' no more."

"They ain't, but they maw sho is. Jus lissen to her."

"Don't pay her no min'. She's always squawkin'. Jus like Aunt Kate," he said.

"Lemme hol' one of them li'l biddies, hear, Riley?"

Riley hesitated, then handed Buster a chick.

"If yuh wasn't so scaired, yuh could go git yuh some," he said.

"Look at him, Riley. He's scaired without his mama!"

"Yeah, yeah. Don't be afraid, li'l feller," cooed Riley. "We yo friends."

"Maybe it's too hot up here. Maybe we better take 'em down," said Buster.

"Saaay! We can teach these li'l son-of-a-guns to fly!"

"I never seen a li'l chicken fly," said Buster skeptically.

"Well, they 'bout the size of a chee-chee bird," said Riley.

"But they ain't got no long wings like a chee-chee bird."

"Hecks, thass right," he said disappointedly. If they wings wuz jus a li'l longer—like the li'l robin's, he thought.

"Hey! Look whut mine kin do," yelled Buster.

He saw Buster place the chick on the ridge of his leg and the little chick flex its wings as it hopped off to the roof.

"He wuz tryin' to fly," he yelled. "These li'l guys wants to fly and they wings ain't strong enough yit!"

"Thass right," agreed Buster. "He wuz really tryin' to fly!"

"I'm gon *make* 'em fly," said Riley.

"How, man?"

"With a parachute!"

"Shoots, ain't no parachute that little."

"Sho there is. We kin make one outa a rag and some string. Then these li'l guys kin go sailing down to their ma," said Riley, making a falling leaf of his hand.

"Suppose they gits hurt and Aunt Kate tells yo mama?"

Riley looked toward the house. Aunt Kate was nowhere to be seen. He looked at the chicks.

"Aw, yuh jus scaired," he taunted Buster.

"Naw I ain't neither. I jus don't want to see 'em hurt, thass all."

"It won't hurt 'em, man. They'll like it. All birds likes to fly, man, even chickens. Jus looka yonder!" he broke off, pointing.

A flock of pigeons circled a distant red brick chimney, dazzling the sunlight with their wings.

"Ain't that something, man?"

"But them's *pigeons,* Riley . . ."

"That ain't nothin'," said Riley, bouncing the chick gently

in his palm. "We kin make 'em go sailing down and down and down and down!"

"But we ain't got no cloth," protested Buster.

Riley bent, taking the cloth where Ole Bill had torn his shirt, pulled it taut and ripped it away. He held the blue piece triumphantly before Buster's face.

"Here's the cloth, right here!"

Buster squirmed. "But we ain't got no string."

"Oh, I got string," said Riley. "I got string and ever'thin."

He fished a ball of twine out of his pocket and held it lovingly. Yesterday he had watched the twine snap with a kite sailing high above the rooftops, and the kite had gone jerking and swooping crazily out of sight, and he had felt that same strange tightness he knew watching the birds fly south in the fall.

"Man, looka there . . ." said Buster, awe in his voice.

A delicate curtain of flesh covered the chick's eye, making it look dead. He paused, about to tie a knot. Then the beady black eyes were open again. Sighing, he held up the cloth, seeing the strings stream lazily in the wind.

"Come on, man. We ready to make these li'l ole guys fly like chee-chee birds."

He paused, looking at the circling pigeons.

"Buster, don't yuh wish somebody would teach yuh an' me how to fly?"

"Well, maybe," Buster said guardedly, "I guess I would. But we needs two parachutes for these here aviators. How yuh gonna make 'em both fly with jus one?"

"Yuh jus hold 'em an' watch ole papa fix it." Riley grinned.

As Buster held the chicks, Riley hitched them together with a harness of twine, then tied them to the parachute strings.

"Now yuh jus watch," he said. He grasped the cloth in its center and raised it gently, swinging the chicks clear of the roof. They peeped excitedly. Buster grinned.

"Come on, man."

They crawled to the edge and looked down. A hen sang a lazy song. A distant rooster challenged the morning and Ole Bill screamed an answer.

"Riley . . ." began Buster.

"Now whut's the matter?"

"Suppose ole Aunt Kate sees us?"

"Hecks, how come yuh have to start thinkin' 'bout her? She's inside talkin' to her Jesus."

"Well—" Buster said.

They sat on the edge now, their legs dangling. Riley trembled with anticipation.

"Yuh want to go down an' bring 'em back?"

"That rooster's still down there, man," said Buster.

Shaking his head in mock hopelessness, Riley clambered down and entered the yard.

Ole Bill clucked a warning from a far corner.

"Les do it like they do in them airplane movies," yelled Buster. "Switch on!"

"Well, switch on then!" Buster yelled.

"Contact!"

"Contact! It's a nonstop flight, man."

"Well, let 'em come down!" yelled Riley impatiently.

Then he was seeing Buster tossing the chicks and parachute into the air, seeing the cloth billow out umbrella-like as the chicks peeped excitedly underneath; seeing it sail slowly down, slowly, like fluff from a cottonwood tree.

"Git down from there, suh!!!"

He whirled, his body tense. Aunt Kate was coming across

the yard. He was poised, like a needle caught between two magnets.

"Riley! Catch 'em!"

He turned, seeing the parachute deflating like a bag of wind and the chicks diving the cloth earthward like a yellow piece of rock. He tried to run to catch the chicks and found himself standing still and hearing Buster and Aunt Kate yelling. Then he was stumbling to where the chicks lay hidden beneath the cloth. Please God, please, he breathed. But when he lifted the chicks, they made no sound and their heads wobbled lifelessly. He dropped slowly to his knees.

A shadow fell across the earth and grew. Looking around, he saw two huge black bunion-shaped shoes. It was Aunt Kate, wheezing noisily.

"Ah tole yuh, suh! Ah knowed yuh'd be into trouble 'fore the day was done! Whut kina devilment yuh up to now?"

He swallowed, his mouth dry.

"Yuh heah me talkin' to yuh, boy!"

"We wuz jus playin'."

"Playin' whut? Whut yuh doin' in there?"

"We . . . we wuz playin flyin' . . ."

"Flyin' the dickens!" she yelled suspiciously. "Lemme see under that there rag!"

"It's jus a piece a rag."

"Lemme see!"

He lifted the cloth. The chicks were heavy as lead. He closed his eyes.

"Ah knowed it! Yuh been killin' off yo ma's chickens!" she shouted. "An' Ahm gon tell her, sho as mah name's Kate."

He stared at her mutely.

If only he hadn't looked when she called, he might have caught the li'l chicks.

Suddenly the words rushed out, scalding: "I hate yuh," he screamed. "I wish yuh had died back in slavery times . . ."

Her face shrank, turning a dirty gray. She was proud of being old. He felt a cold blast of fear.

"The Lawd's gonna punish yuh in hellfire for that," she said brokenly. "Someday yuh remember them words an' moan an' cry."

There, she'd done put a curse on him. He felt pebbles cutting into his knees as he watched her turn and go. She padded painfully away, her head shaking indignantly, her white apron stiff over her wide, gingham-covered hips.

"These li'l nineteen hundred young'uns is jus full of the devil, that whut they is," she muttered. "Jus full of the devil."

For a long time he stared vacantly at the chicks lying upon the earth strewn with the chalk-green droppings of the fowls. The old hen circled cautiously before him, pleading noisily for her children. Fighting a sense of loathing, he lifted the chicks, removed the strings, and laid them down again . . .

For a little while they were flying . . .

Buster looked sorrowfully through the fence. "I'm sorry, Riley," he said.

Riley did not answer. Suddenly aware of the foul odor of chicken dung, he stood, feeling the waxy smear upon his exposed flesh as he absently wiped his fingers.

If I jus hadn't looked at her, he thought. His eyes swam. And so great was his anguish he did not hear the swift rush of feathers or see the brilliant flash of outspread wings as Ole Bill charged. The blow staggered him, and looking down, he saw with tear-filled eyes the bright red stream against the brown where the spur had torn his leg.

"We almost had 'em flyin'," said Riley. "We almost . . ."

A Coupla Scalped Indians

They had a small, loud-playing band and as we moved through the trees I could hear the notes of the horns bursting like bright metallic bubbles against the sky. It was a faraway and sparklike sound, shooting through the late afternoon quiet of the hill; very clear now and definitely music, band music. I was relieved. I had been hearing it for several minutes as we moved through the woods, but the pain down there had made all my senses so deceptively sharp that I had decided that the sound was simply a musical ringing in my ears. But now I was doubly sure, for Buster stopped and looked at me, squinching up his eyes with his head cocked to one side. He was wearing a blue

From *New World Writing,* 1956

cloth headband with a turkey feather stuck over his ear, and I could see it flutter in the breeze.

"You hear what I hear, man?" he said.

"I *been* hearing it," I said.

"Damn! We better haul it outa these woods so we can see something. Why didn't you say something to a man?"

We moved again, hurrying along until suddenly we were out of the woods, standing at a point of the hill where the path dropped down to the town, our eyes searching. It was close to sundown and below me I could see the red clay of the path cutting through the woods and moving past a white lightning-blasted tree to join the river road, and the narrow road shifting past Aunt Mackie's old shack, and on, beyond the road and the shack, I could see the dull mysterious movement of the river. The horns were blasting brighter now, though still far away, sounding like somebody flipping bright handfuls of new small change against the sky. I listened and followed the river swiftly with my eyes as it wound through the trees and on past the buildings and houses of the town—until there, there at the farther edge of the town, past the tall smokestack and the great silver sphere of the gas storage tower, floated the tent, spread white and cloudlike with its bright ropes of fluttering flags.

That's when we started running. It was a dogtrotting Indian run, because we were both wearing packs and were tired from the tests we had been taking in the woods and in Indian Lake. But now the bright blare of the horns made us forget our tiredness and pain and we bounded down the path like young goats in the twilight; our army-surplus mess kits and canteens rattling against us.

"We late, man," Buster said. "I told you we was gon fool

around and be late. But naw, you had to cook that damn sage hen with mud on him just like it says in the book. We coulda barbecued a damn elephant while we was waiting for a tough sucker like that to get done. . . ."

His voice grumbled on like a trombone with a big, fat pot-shaped mute stuck in it and I ran on without answering. We had tried to take the cooking test by using a sage hen instead of a chicken because Buster said Indians didn't eat chicken. So we'd taken time to flush a sage hen and kill him with a slingshot. Besides, he was the one who insisted that we try the running endurance test, the swimming test, *and* the cooking test all in one day. Sure it had taken time. I knew it would take time, especially with our having no scoutmaster. We didn't even have a troop, only the *Boy Scout's Handbook* that Buster had found, and—as we'd figured—our hardest problem had been working out the tests for ourselves. He had no right to argue anyway, since he'd beaten me in all the tests—although I'd passed them too. And he was the one who insisted that we start taking them today, even though we were both still sore and wearing our bandages, and I was still carrying some of the catgut stitches around in me. I had wanted to wait a few days until I was healed, but Mister Know-it-all Buster challenged me by saying that a real stud Indian could take the tests even right after the doctor had just finished sewing on him. So, since we were more interested in being *Indian* scouts than simply *Boy* Scouts, here I was running toward the spring carnival instead of being already there. I wondered how Buster knew so much about what an Indian would do, anyway. We certainly hadn't read anything about what the doctor had done to us. He'd probably made it up, and I had let him urge me into going to the woods even though I had to slip out of the house. The doctor had told Miss Janey (she's the lady who takes care of me) to keep me quiet for a few days and she dead-aimed to do it. You would've thought from the way she carried on that she was the one who had the operation—only that's one kind of operation no woman ever gets to brag about.

Anyway, Buster and me had been in the woods and now we were plunging down the hill through the fast-falling dark to the carnival. I had begun to throb and the bandage was chafing, but as we rounded a curve I could see the tent and the flares and the gathering crowd. There was a breeze coming up the hill against us now and I could almost smell that cotton candy, the hamburgers, and the kerosene smell of the flares. We stopped to rest and Buster stood very straight and pointed down below, making a big sweep with his arm like an Indian chief in the movies when he's up on a hill telling his braves and the Great Spirit that he's getting ready to attack a wagon train.

"Heap big . . . teepee . . . down yonder," he said in Indian talk. "Smoke signal say . . . Blackfeet . . . make . . . heap much . . . stink, buck-dancing in tennis shoes!"

"Ugh," I said, bowing my suddenly war-bonneted head. "Ugh!"

Buster swept his arm from east to west, his face impassive. "Smoke medicine say . . . heap . . . *big* stink! Hot toe jam!" He struck his palm with his fist, and I looked at his puffed-out cheeks and giggled.

"Smoke medicine say you tell heap big lie," I said. "Let's get on down there."

We ran past some trees, Buster's canteen jangling. Around us it was quiet except for the roosting birds.

"Man," I said, "you making as much noise as a team of mules in full harness. Don't no Indian scout make all that racket when he runs."

"No scout-um now," he said. "Me go make heap much pow-wow at stinky-dog carnival!"

"Yeah, but you'll get yourself scalped, making all that noise in the woods," I said. "Those other Indians don't give a damn 'bout no carnival—what does a carnival mean to them? They'll scalp the hell outa you!"

"Scalp?" he said, talking colored now. "Hell, man—that damn doctor scalped me last week. Damn near took my whole head off!"

I almost fell with laughing. "Have mercy, Lord," I laughed. "We're just a couple poor scalped Indians!"

Buster stumbled about, grabbing a tree for support. The doctor had said that it would make us men and Buster had said, hell, he was a man already—what he wanted was to be an Indian. We hadn't thought about it making us scalped ones.

"You right, man," Buster said. "Since he done scalped so much of my head away, I must be crazy as a fool. That's why I'm in such a hurry to get down yonder with the other crazy folks. I want to be right in the middle of 'em when they really start raising hell."

"Oh, you'll be there, Chief Baldhead," I said.

He looked at me blankly. "What you think ole Doc done with our scalps?"

"Made him a tripe stew, man."

"You nuts," Buster said. "He probably used 'em for fish bait."

"He did, I'm going to sue him for one trillion, zillion dollars, cash," I said.

"Maybe he gave 'em to ole Aunt Mackie, man. I bet with them she could work up some out*rageous* spells!"

"Man," I said, suddenly shivering, "don't talk about that old woman, she's evil."

"Hell, everybody's so scared of her. I just wish she'd mess with me or my daddy, I'd fix her."

I said nothing—I was afraid. For though I had seen the old woman about town all my life, she remained to me like the moon, mysterious in her very familiarity; and in the sound of her name there was terror:

Ho' Aunt Mackie, talker-with-spirits, prophetess-of-disaster, odd-dweller-alone in a riverside shack surrounded by sun-flowers, morning-glories, and strange magical weeds (Yao, as Buster, during our Indian phase, would have put it, Yao!); *Old Aunt Mackie, wizen-faced walker-with-a-stick, shrill-voiced ranter in the night, round-eyed malicious one, given to dramatic trances and fiery flights of rage; Aunt Mackie, preacher of wild sermons on the busy streets of the town, hot-voiced chaser of children, snuff-dipper, visionary; wearer of greasy headrags, wrinkled gingham aprons, and old men's shoes; Aunt Mackie, nobody's sister but still Aunt Mackie to us all* (Ho, Yao!); *teller of fortunes, concocter of powerful, body-rending spells* (Yah, Yao!); *Aunt Mackie, the remote one though always seen about us; night-consulted adviser to farmers on crops and cattle* (Yao!); *herb-healer, root-doctor, and town-confounding oracle to wildcat drillers seeking oil in the earth*—(Yaaaah-Ho!). It was all there in her name and before her name I shivered. Once uttered, for me the palaver was finished; I resigned it to Buster, the tough one.

Even some of the grown folks, both black and white, were afraid of Aunt Mackie, and all the kids except Buster. Buster lived on the outskirts of the town and was as unimpressed by Aunt Mackie as by the truant officer and others whom the rest of us regarded with awe. And because I was his buddy I was ashamed of my fear.

Usually I had extra courage when I was with him. Like the time two years before when we had gone into the woods with only our slingshots, a piece of fatback, and a skillet and had lived three days on the rabbits we killed and the wild berries we picked and the ears of corn we raided from farmers' fields. We slept each rolled in his quilt, and in the night Buster had told bright stories of the world we'd find when we were grown-up and gone from hometown and family. I had no family, only Miss Janey, who took me after my mother died (I didn't know my father), so that getting away always appealed to me, and the coming time of which Buster liked to talk loomed in the darkness around me, rich with pastel promise. And although we heard a bear go lumbering through the woods nearby and the eerie howling of a coyote in the dark, yes, and had been swept by the soft swift flight of an owl, Buster was unafraid and I had grown brave in the grace of his courage.

But to me Aunt Mackie was a threat of a different order, and I paid her the respect of fear.

"Listen to those horns," Buster said. And now the sound came through the trees like colored marbles glinting in the summer sun.

We ran again. And now keeping pace with Buster I felt good; for I meant to be there too, at the carnival; right in the middle of all that confusion and sweating and laughing and all the strange sights to see.

"Listen to 'em, now, man," Buster said. "Those fools is

starting to shout 'Amazing Grace' on those horns. Let's step on the gas!"

The scene danced below us as we ran. Suddenly there was a towering Ferris wheel revolving slowly out of the dark, its red and blue lights glowing like drops of dew dazzling a big spider web when you see it in the early morning. And we heard the beckoning blare of the band now shot through with the small, insistent, buckshot voices of the barkers.

"Listen to that trombone, man," I said.,

"Sounds like he's playing the dozens with the whole wide world."

"What's he saying, Buster?"

"He's saying. 'Ya'll's mamas don't wear 'em. Is strictly without 'em. Don't know nothing 'bout 'em . . ."

"Don't know about what, man?"

"Draw's, fool; he's talking 'bout draw's!"

"How you know, man?"

"I hear him talking, don't I?"

"Sure, but you been scalped, remember? You crazy. How he know about those people's mamas?" I said.

"Says he saw 'em with his great big ole eye."

"Damn! He must be a Peeping Tom. How about those other horns?"

"Now that there tuba's saying:

" '*They don't play 'em, I know they don't.*
They don't play 'em, I know they won't.
They just don't play no nasty dirty twelves . . .' "

"Man, you *are* a scalped-headed fool. How about that trumpet?"

"Him? That fool's a soldier, he's really signifying. Saying,

> " *'So ya'll don't play 'em, hey?*
> *So ya'll won't play 'em, hey?*
> *Well pat your feet and clap your hands,*
> *'Cause I'm going to play 'em to the promised land . . .'*

"Man, the white folks know what that fool is signifying on that horn they'd run him clear on out the world. Trumpet's got a real *nasty* mouth."

"Why you call him a soldier, man?" I said.

" 'Cause he's slipping 'em in the twelves and choosing 'em, all at the same time. Talking 'bout they mamas and offering to fight 'em. Now he ain't like that ole clarinet; clarinet so sweet-talking he just *eases* you in the dozens."

"Say, Buster," I said, seriously now. "You know, we gotta stop cussing and playing the dozens if we're going to be Boy Scouts. Those white boys don't play that mess."

"You doggone right they don't," he said, the turkey feather vibrating above his ear. "Those guys can't take it, man. Besides, who wants to be just like them? Me, *I'm* gon be a scout and play the twelves too! You have to, with some of these old jokers we know. You don't know what to say when they start teasing you, you never have no peace. You have to outtalk 'em, outrun 'em, or outfight 'em and I don't aim to be running and fighting all the time. N'mind those white boys."

We moved on through the growing dark. Already I could see a few stars and suddenly there was the moon. It emerged bladelike from behind a thin veil of cloud, just as I heard a new sound and looked about me with quick uneasiness. Off to our left I heard a dog, a big one. I slowed, seeing the outlines of a picket fence and the odd-shaped shadows that lurked in Aunt Mackie's yard.

"What's the matter, man?" Buster said.

"Listen," I said. "That's Aunt Mackie's dog. Last year I was passing here and he sneaked up and bit me through the fence when I wasn't even thinking about him . . ."

"Hush, man," Buster whispered, "I hear the son-of-a-bitch back in there now. You leave him to me."

We moved by inches now, hearing the dog barking in the dark. Then we were going past and he was throwing his heavy body against the fence, straining at his chain. We hesitated, Buster's hand on my arm. I undid my heavy canteen belt and held it, suddenly light in my fingers. In my right I gripped the hatchet which I'd brought along.

"We'd better go back and take the other path," I whispered.

"Just stand still, man," Buster said.

The dog hit the fence again, barking hoarsely; and in the interval following the echoing crash I could hear the distant music of the band.

"Come on," I said. "Let's go round."

"Hell, no! We're going straight! I ain't letting no damn dog scare me, Aunt Mackie or no Aunt Mackie. Come on!"

Trembling, I moved with him toward the roaring dog, then felt him stop again, and I could hear him removing his pack and taking out something wrapped in paper.

"Here," he said. "You take my stuff and come on."

I took his gear and went behind him, hearing his voice suddenly hot with fear and anger saying, "Here, you 'gator-mouthed egg-sucker, see how you like this sage hen," just as I tripped over the straps of his pack and went down. Then I was crawling frantically, trying to untangle myself and hearing the dog growling as he crunched something in his jaws. "Eat it, you buzzard," Buster was saying, "see if you tough as he is," as I tried to stand, stumbling and sending an old cooking range crashing in the dark. Part of the fence was gone and in my panic I had crawled into the yard. Now I could hear the dog bark threateningly and leap the length of his chain toward me, then back to the sage hen; toward me, a swift leaping form snatched backward by the heavy chain, turning to mouth savagely on the mangled bird. Moving away, I floundered over the stove and pieces of crating, against giant sunflower stalks, trying to get back to Buster, when I saw the lighted window and realized that I had crawled to the very shack itself. That's when I pressed against the weathered-satin side of the shack and came erect. And there, framed by the window in the lamp-lit room, I saw the woman.

A brown naked woman, whose black hair hung beneath her shoulders. I could see the long graceful curve of her back as she moved in some sort of slow dance, bending forward and back, her arms and body moving as though gathering in something which I couldn't see but which she drew to her with pleasure; a young, girlish body with slender, well-rounded hips. *But who?* flashed through my mind as I heard Buster's *Hey, man; where'd you go? You done run out on me?* from back in the dark. And I willed to move, to hurry away—but in that instant she chose to pick up a glass from a wobbly old round white table and to drink, turning slowly as she stood with backward-tilted head, slowly turning in the lamplight and drinking slowly as she turned, slowly; until I could see the full-faced glowing of her feminine form.

And I was frozen there, watching the uneven movement of her breasts beneath the glistening course of the liquid, spilling down her body in twin streams drawn by the easy tiding of her breathing. Then the glass came down and my knees flowed beneath me like water. The air seemed to explode soundlessly. I shook my head but she, the image, would not go away and I wanted suddenly to laugh wildly and to scream. For above the smooth shoulders of the girlish form I saw the wrinkled face of old Aunt Mackie.

Now, I had never seen a naked woman before, only very little girls or once or twice a skinny one my own age, who looked like a boy with the boy part missing. And even though I'd seen a few calendar drawings they were not alive like this, nor images of someone you'd thought familiar through having seen them passing through the streets of the town; nor like this inconsistent, with wrinkled face mismatched with glowing form. So that mixed with my fear of punishment for peeping there was added the terror of her mystery. And yet I could not move away. I was fascinated, hearing the growling dog and feeling a warm pain grow beneath my bandage—along with the newly risen terror that this deceptive old woman could cause me to feel this way, that she could be so young beneath her old baggy clothes.

She was dancing again now, still unaware of my eyes, the lamplight playing on her body as she swayed and enfolded the air or invisible ghosts or whatever it was within her arms. Each time she moved, her hair, which was black as night now that it was no longer hidden beneath a greasy headrag, swung heavily about her shoulders. And as she moved to the side I could see the gentle tossing of her breasts beneath her upraised arms. *It just can't be,* I thought, *it just can't,* and moved closer, determined to see and to know. But I had forgotten the hatchet in my hand until it struck the side of the house and I saw her turn quickly toward the window, her face evil as she swayed. I was rigid as stone, hearing the growling dog mangling the bird and knowing that I should run even as she moved toward the window, her shadow flying before her, her hair now wild as snakes writhing on a dead tree during a springtime flood. Then I could hear Buster's hoarse-voiced *Hey, man! Where in hell are you?* even as she pointed at me and screamed, sending me moving backward, and I was aware of the sickle-shaped moon flying like a lightning flash as I fell, still gripping my hatchet, and struck my head in the dark.

When I started out of it someone was holding me and I lay in light and looked up to see her face above me. Then it all flooded swiftly back and I was aware again of the contrast between smooth body and wrinkled face and experienced a sudden warm yet painful thrill. She held me close. Her breath came to me, sweetly alcoholic as she mumbled something about "Little devil, lips that touch wine shall never touch mine! That's what I told him, understand me? Never," she said loudly. "You understand?"

"Yes, ma'm . . ."

"Never, never, NEVER!"

"No, ma'm," I said, seeing her study me with narrowed eyes.

"You young but you young'uns understand, devilish as you is. What you doing messing round in my yard?"

"I got lost," I said. "I was coming from taking some Boy Scout tests and I was trying to get by your dog."

"So that's what I heard," she said. "He bite you?"

"No, ma'm."

"Corse not, he don't bite on the new moon. No, I think you come in my yard to spy on me."

"No, ma'm, I didn't," I said. "I just happened to see the light when I was stumbling around trying to find my way."

"You got a pretty big hatchet there," she said, looking down at my hand. "What you plan to do with it?"

"It's a kind of Boy Scout ax," I said. "I used it to come through the woods . . ."

She looked at me dubiously. "So," she said, "you're a heavy hatchet man and you stopped to peep. Well, what I want to know is, is you a drinking man? Have your lips ever touched wine?"

"Wine? No, ma'm."

"So you ain't a drinking man, but do you belong to church?"

"Yes, ma'm."

"And have you been saved and ain't no backslider?"

"Yessum."

"Well," she said, pursing her lips, "I guess you can kiss me."

"MA'M?"

"That's what I said. You passed all the tests and you was peeping in my window . . ."

She was holding me there on a cot, her arms around me as though I were a three-year-old, smiling like a girl. I could see her fine white teeth and the long hairs on her chin and it was like a bad dream. "You peeped," she said, "now you got to do the rest. I said kiss me, or I'll fix you . . ."

I saw her face come close and felt her warm breath and closed my eyes, trying to force myself. *It's just like kissing some sweaty woman at church,* I told myself, *some friend of Miss Janey's.* But it didn't help and I could feel her drawing me and I found her lips with mine. It was dry and firm and winey and I could hear her sigh. "Again," she said, and once more my lips found hers. And suddenly she drew me to her and I could feel her breasts soft against me as once more she sighed.

"That was a nice boy," she said, her voice kind, and I opened my eyes. "That's enough now, you're both too young and too old, but you're brave. A regular li'l chocolate hero."

And now she moved and I realized for the first time that my hand had found its way to her breast. I moved it guiltily, my face flaming as she stood.

"You're a good brave boy," she said, looking at me from deep in her eyes, "but you forget what happened here tonight."

I sat up as she stood looking down upon me with a mysterious smile. And I could see her body up close now, in the dim yellow light; see the surprising silkiness of black hair mixed here and there with gray, and suddenly I was crying and hating myself for the compelling need. I looked at my hatchet lying on the floor now and wondered how she'd gotten me into the shack as the tears blurred my eyes.

"What's the matter, boy?" she said. And I had no words to answer.

"What's the matter, I say!"

"I'm hurting in my operation," I said desperately, knowing that my tears were too complicated to put into any words I knew.

"Operation? Where?"

I looked away.

"Where you hurting, boy?" she demanded.

I looked into her eyes and they seemed to flood through me, until reluctantly I pointed toward my pain.

"Open it, so's I can see," she said. "You know I'm a healer, don't you?"

I bowed my head, still hesitating.

"Well open it then. How'm I going to see with all those clothes on you?"

My face burned like fire now and the pain seemed to ease as a dampness grew beneath the bandage. But she would not be denied and I undid myself and saw a red stain on the gauze. I lay there ashamed to raise my eyes.

"Hmmmmmmm," she said. "A fishing worm with a headache!" And I couldn't believe my ears. Then she was looking into my eyes and grinning.

"Pruned," she cackled in her high, old woman's voice, "pruned. Boy, you have been pruned. I'm a doctor but no tree surgeon—no, lay still a second."

She paused and I saw her hand come forward, three clawlike fingers taking me gently as she examined the bandage.

And I was both ashamed and angry and now I stared at her out of a quick resentment and a defiant pride. *I'm a man,* I said within myself. *Just the same I am a man!* But I could only stare at her face briefly as she looked at me with a gleam in her eyes. Then my eyes fell and I forced myself to look boldly at her now, very brown in the lamplight, with all the complicated apparatus within the globular curvatures of flesh and vessel exposed to my eyes. I was filled then with a deeper sense of the mystery of it too, for now it was as though the nakedness was nothing more than another veil; much like the old baggy dresses she always wore. Then across the curvature of her stomach I saw a long, puckered crescent-shaped scar.

"How old are you, boy?" she said, her eyes suddenly round.

"Eleven," I said. And it was as though I had fired a shot.

"Eleven! Git out of here," she screamed, stumbling backward, her eyes wide upon me as she felt for the glass on the table to drink. Then she snatched an old gray robe from a chair, fumbling for the tie cord which wasn't there. I moved, my eyes upon her as I knelt for my hatchet, and felt the pain come sharp. Then I straightened, trying to arrange my knickers.

"You go now, you little rascal," she said. "Hurry and git out of here. And if I ever hear of you saying anything about me I'll fix your daddy and your mammy too. I'll fix 'em, you hear?"

"Yes, ma'm," I said, feeling that I had suddenly lost the courage of my manhood, now that my bandage was hidden and her secret body gone behind her old gray robe. But how could she fix my father when I didn't have one? Or my mother, when she was dead?

I moved, backing out of the door into the dark. Then she slammed the door and I saw the light grow intense in the window and there was her face looking out at me and I could not tell if she frowned or smiled, but in the glow of the lamp the wrinkles were not there. I stumbled over the packs now and gathered them up, leaving.

This time the dog raised up, huge in the dark, his green eyes glowing as he gave me a low disinterested growl. *Buster really must have fixed you,* I thought. *But where'd he go?* Then I was past the fence into the road.

I wanted to run but was afraid of starting the pain again, and as I moved I kept seeing her as she'd appeared with her back turned toward me, the sweet undrunken movements that she made. It had been like someone dancing by herself and yet like praying without kneeling down. Then she had turned, exposing her familiar face. I moved faster now and suddenly all my senses seemed to sing alive. I heard a night bird's song; the lucid call of a quail arose. And from off to my right in the river there came the leap of a moon-mad fish and I could see the spray arch up and away. There was wisteria in the air and the scent of moonflowers. And now moving through the dark I recalled the warm, intriguing smell of her body and suddenly, with the shout of the carnival coming to me again, the whole thing became thin and dreamlike. The images flowed in my mind, became shadowy; no part was left to fit another. But still there was my pain and here was I, running through the dark toward the small, loud-playing band. It was real, I knew, and I stopped in the path and looked back, seeing the black outlines of the shack and the thin moon above. Behind the shack the hill arose with the shadowy woods and I knew the lake was still hidden there, reflecting the moon. All was real.

And for a moment I felt much older, as though I had lived swiftly long years into the future and had been as swiftly pushed back again. I tried to remember how it had been when I kissed her, but on my lips my tongue found only the faintest trace of wine. But for that it was gone, and I thought forever, except the memory of the scraggly hairs on her chin. Then I was again aware of the imperious calling of the horns and moved again toward the carnival. Where was that other scalped Indian; where had Buster gone?

Hymie's Bull

We were just drifting; going no place in particular, having long ago given up hopes of finding jobs. We were just knocking around the country. [Just drifting, ten black boys on an L&N freight.] From Birmingham we had swung up to the world's fair at Chicago, where the bull had met us in the yards and turned us around and knocked a few lumps on our heads as souvenirs. If you've ever had a bull stand so close he can't miss, and hit you across the rump as you crawled across the top of a boxcar and when you tried to get out of the way, because you knew he had a gun as well as a loaded stick, you've had him measure a tender spot on your head and let go with his loaded stick like a man cracking black walnuts with a hammer; and if when you started to climb down the side of the car because you didn't want to jump from the moving train like he said, you've had him step on your fingers with his heavy boots and grind them with his heel like you'd do a cockroach and then if you didn't let go, he beat you across the knuckles with his loaded stick till you did let go; and when you did, you hit the cinders and found yourself tumbling and sliding on your face away from the train faster than the telephone poles alongside the tracks, then you can understand why we were glad as hell we only had a few lumps on the head. Especially when you remember that the Chicago bulls hate black bums 'bout as much as Texas Slim, who'll kill a Negro as quick as he'll crack down on a blackbird sitting on a fence.

Bulls are pretty bad people to meet if you're a bum. They have head-whipping down to a science and they're always ready to go into action. They know all the places to hit to change a bone into jelly, and they seem to feel just the place to kick you to make your backbone feel like it's going to fold up like the old collapsible drinking cups we used when we were kids. Once a bull hit me across the bridge of my nose and I felt like I was coming apart like a cigarette floating in a urinal. They can hit you on your head and bust your shoes.

But sometimes the bulls get the worst of it, and whenever one is missing at the end of a run and they find him all cut up and bleeding, they start taking all the black boys off the freights. Most of the time, they don't care who did it, because the main thing is to make some black boy pay for it. Now when you hear that we're the only bums that carry knives you can just put that down as bull talk because what I'm fixing to tell you about was done by an ofay bum named Hymie from Brooklyn.

We were riding a manifest, and Hymie was sick from some bad grub he'd bummed in a little town a few miles back when the freight had stopped for water. Maybe it wasn't the grub; maybe it was the old mulligan pot he'd cooked it in back there in the jungle. We liked that spot because sunflowers grew there and gave plenty of shade from the sun. But anyway, Hymie was sick and riding on top. It was hot and the flies kept swarming into the car so fast that we stopped paying them no mind. Hymie must have caught hell from them though because his dinner kept coming up and splattering the air. He must have been plenty bothered with the flies because we could see his dinner fly past the door of the car where we were. Once it was very red like a cardinal flying past in the green fields along the tracks. Come to think of it, it might have been a cardinal flying past. Or it might have been something else that smelled like swill from a farmyard.

We tried to get the guy to come down, but he said that he felt better out in the air, so we left him alone. In fact we started to play blackjack for cigarette butts and soon forgot about Hymie; that is, until it had gotten too dark in the boxcar to see the spots on the cards. Then I decided to go out on top to watch the sunset.

The sun was a big globe in the west that seemed to drop away like a basketball tossed into a basket, and the freight seemed to be trying to catch it before it got there. You could see large swarms of flies following the freight cars like gulls over a boat; only the noise *they* made was lost in the roar of the train. In the field you could see a flock of birds flying away into the sunset, shooting off at an angle to rise and dip, rise and dip, sail and pivot in the wind like kites cut loose from their strings.

I stood on top, feeling the wind pushing against my eyes and whipping my pants against my legs, and waved to Hymie. He had his legs locked around the open ventilator of a refrigerator car hooked next to ours. In that light he looked like a fellow propped in a corner with his hands and feet tied like in a gangster picture. I waved to Hymie, and he waved back. It was a weak wave. The train was going downgrade now, and the fields passed in a curve, and it made you feel like you were on a merry-go-round. When you tried to holler, your voice was small, like the sound you heard when you used to sit on the bottom of the swimming hole and knock rocks together. So we, Hymie and me, just waved.

I felt sorry for the poor guy out there alone. I wished there was something I could do for him, but they don't have water on side-door Pullmans and I guess bums are too dumb to carry canteens. Then I thought, To heck with Hymie. A few miles down the road when we got South, he and the other guys would go into another car anyway.

I stood there on top listening to the rhythm of the wheels bumping along the tracks. Sometimes the rhythm was even, like kids in Harlem beating empty boxes around a bonfire at nightfall as they play along the curbs. I stood there on top listening, bent slightly forward to keep my balance like a guy skiing, and thought of my mother. I had left her two months before, not even knowing that I would ever hop freights. Poor Mama, she had tried hard to keep my brother and me at home, but she fed us too long alone, and we were getting much too grown-up to let her do it any longer, so we left home looking for jobs.

It was now becoming almost too dark to see, when all at once the freight gave a jerk, and every boxcar in the train started racing every other car bumpty-bump down the tracks to the engine like they were meant to knock it into a faster speed when they got there. Then I looked down to where Hymie was riding, and there was a bull crawling toward him with a stick in his hand. I hollered for Hymie to watch out, but the noise swallowed up my voice and the bull was drawing closer all the time. You see, Hymie was asleep, his legs still locked around the ventilator, when the bull reached him. Then the bull grabs Hymie to yank him up and starts lamming with his stick at the same time. Hymie woke up fighting and yelling; I could see his face. The stick would land, and a scream would drift back to where I crawled, almost too excited to move. The freight streaked along like a long black dog, and up on top we were like three monkeys clinging to his back, like you see sometimes at a circus. The bull finally got his knees on Hymie's chest and was choking him, the stick hanging from his wrist by a leather thong.

Sometimes he tried to break Hymie's hold to throw him off the car, and sometimes he lammed away with the loaded stick. Hymie fought the bull the best he could, but he fumbled in his pocket with one hand at the same time. You could see the bull hit, measure and hit, and Hymie kept his left hand in the bull's face and all the time he was fumbling in his pocket.

Then I saw something flash in the fast-fading light, and Hymie went into action with his blade. The bull was still hammering away with his stick when Hymie started cutting him aloose. You could see the knife flash up past Hymie's head and then dive down and across both the bull's wrists, and you could hear him scream because all the time you were coming closer and you could see him let Hymie go and

Hymie raise himself, swing the blade around in half circles like a snake and the blade swing back around as though measuring just the right spot, then dive into the bull's throat. Hymie pulled the knife around from ear to ear in the bull's throat; then he stabbed him and pushed him off the top of the car. The bull paused a second in the air like a kid diving off a trestle into a river, then hit the cinders below. Something was warm on my face, and I found that some of the bull's blood had blown back like spray when a freight stops to take on water from a tank.

It was dark now, and Hymie tore off his top shirt, and dropped it over the edge of the car, and crawled down the side. He hung there until the train hit an upgrade and slowed down. We were coming to a little town on a hill. Lights were scattered here and there like raisins in a cake, and drawing nearer I saw Hymie grow tense and fall clear of the car. He hit the dirt hard, rolled a few yards, and got up to his feet. By then we were too far gone to see him in the dim light. We rolled past the little town, and the whistle screamed its lonely sound and I wondered if that was the last I'd see of Hymie . . .

I heard later on that the shirt Hymie wore was found caught on a field fence and that his switchblade was still sticking in the bull. The bull had rolled from the cinders into the vines which lined the tracks, and lay there all bloody among the flowers that looked like tiger lilies.

The next day about dusk we were pulling into the yards at Montgomery, Alabama, miles down the line, and got the scare of our lives. The train had to cross a trestle before it could reach the yards. It was going slow, and as soon as it crossed we started getting off. All at once we heard someone hollering, and when we ran up to the front of the freight, there were two bulls, a long one and a short one, fanning heads with their gun barrels. They were making everybody line up so they could see us better. The sky was cloudy and very black. We knew Hymie's bull had been found and some black boy had to go. But luck must've been with us this time because just then the storm broke and the freight started to pull out of the yards. The bulls hollered for no one to get back on the train and we broke and ran between some cars on around to try to catch the freight pulling out at the other end of the yards. We made it. We rode up on top that night out in the rain. It was uncomfortable, but we were happy as hell, and we knew the sun would dry our clothes on us the next day, and we would grab something fast going far away from where Hymie got his bull.

I Did Not Learn Their Names

It was chilly up on top. We were riding to St. Louis on a manifest, clinging to the top of a boxcar. It was dark, and sparks from the engine flew back to where we were riding. Sometimes cinders blew in our faces, and the thick, tumbling part of the blackness was smoke. The freight jerked and bumped, and sparks flew past, dancing red in the whirling darkness. It was chilly as hell, and we were traveling fast. The Santa Fe freight was highballing down a grade in the dark. Miles off to our left, an airport beacon carved the night. Up on top, it was cold for early fall, and the cinders struck our faces like sand awhirl in the wind.

From *The New Yorker,* April 29 & May 6, 1996

"How soon'll we make it to St. Louis?" I yelled to Morrie.

"Tomorrow noon, if she don't jump the track. She's running like a bitch with the itch," he yelled in my ear.

Morrie was my buddy. I had met him in the sunflower jungle outside an Oklahoma town. He climbed off when the freight stopped and sat near me on the embankment. It had given me a queer feeling as I watched him roll up his trousers and take off his leg. The artificial leg had been flesh-white and the stump red and raw. He had lost his leg to the knee beneath the wheels of a freight, and the artificial leg had been given him by an insurance company. He told me he had been on the bum for five years. The next day, he had saved me from falling between two cars to the wheels below, and he got quite a kick out of having a Negro for a buddy.

An old couple was riding in the car below us. I had seen them climb quietly into the boxcar when the freight made its last stop at dusk. I had gone down to see the old man stripping the car of its brown-paper lining to make a bed for the old lady. It was an ingenious thing for him to do. I wondered why no one had thought to do it before. The floor of a boxcar is hard, and the paper used to line the walls of cars in which automobiles are shipped is the softest thing about them. When the freight hit a rough stretch of track, you usually stood up until it was passed. Or else you rested back on the palms of your hands and bounced with the bumps as though your arms were springs. The old man had saved his wife that indignity. It's really a ridiculous position to assume: your hands palm down, your feet flat, and your tail held just high enough off the floor to get it spanked whenever the freight gave a hard jerk and bounced. You usually laughed when you did this, and I could not imagine the old lady in such a position and laughing.

I had gone back on top to join Morrie, but I went off to sleep and he woke me and I crawled down. It was pitch-dark in the car when I climbed down, and I could hear the old lady coughing. She could not sleep for the bumping and the chill. I didn't wish to disturb them, and eased over and sat with my legs dangling out of the open door. I went to sleep that way, watching the lights of distant towns.

The freight started bumping, and I woke to see the line in the east turning red with the dawn. In the dim light, I made out the old man sitting with his back against the side of the car. He was nodding, and the old lady lay in his arms. Then the freight was blowing for a crossing and the whistle sounded lonely in the gray dawn, and I went to sleep again. When I awoke, the sun was in the fields and a flock of sparrows was spurting past the car. I had intended to climb on top before it was light enough for the old couple to see me, but when I got up the old man was watching me from across the car. They were having breakfast.

"Good morning," I said.

He nodded, munching a sandwich.

I stretched and started outside to find Morrie. I was sorry that I hadn't wakened in time to save them embarrassment. In the dark, I was like all the rest who were on the freight and it didn't make a difference. Now it did. I was very sorry. I was having a hard time trying not to hate in those days, and I felt bad whenever I found myself in a position that might have been interpreted that way. I still fought the bums—with Morrie's help. But I had learned not to attack those who were not personally aggressive and who only expressed passively what they had been taught. And these were old folks. She was the oldest woman I'd seen riding the freights, much older than my own mother at home. They seemed kind, and I had not wished to cause them embarrassment.

I was nasty sometimes, because to be decent was to appear afraid and aware of a "place." And since when you were decent they thought that you were afraid, and that you were expressing those qualities that even their schoolbooks said your race possessed, I was almost always nasty. Then Morrie had saved my life, and I tried to change.

As I started to climb up, the old man called me:

"Come here a minute."

Probably wants to cuss me for being here, I thought. Probably thinks he owns the boxcar.

The freight was making a lot of noise, and he motioned for me to sit down. They had sandwiches in a small suitcase, and I sat down in front of it. There were two large red apples in among the sandwiches wrapped in waxed paper. The old lady, seated cross-legged on her brown-paper cushion, looked sadly out on the morning. They were not the kind of people you usually saw on the freights, even in those days.

The old man motioned for me to take a sandwich. I shook my head in refusal, but he insisted. I took the sandwich. I had some grub in Morrie's coat pocket up on top, but he insisted and I was curious and wanted to see what would happen. It was a good sandwich—cold beef with mustard.

"Are you going far?" the old man shouted.

"To Alabama."

Even though he was old and I had been taught to say

"sir," I did not. Saying "sir" was too much a part of knowing your place. I had learned that on the road you really had no place; you were all the same though some of them did not understand that.

The old lady turned and looked at me, silently.

"But Alabama is south," the old man said. "We're traveling *north.*"

"Yes, I know. But this way I'll see part of the country I might not have a chance to see again."

"That's right. It's good for a young fellow to travel."

I was glad he thought so. I had left home to earn money for my school tuition and ended up on the freights.

I had hitchhiked out to Denver and felt the mountains in the morning mist, high and mysterious and psychic before the sun came, as I rode with a family headed for California in an old Ford car. But there had been no work in Denver. I had roamed around. I had gone back to Oklahoma for a while, and later grabbed a freight away. I had gone through the Ozarks, where orange flowers with splashes of red like tiger lilies lined the tracks. Through western Kansas, with the fields bare and buzzards flying and the fields in motion with black-tailed rabbits and blowing dust; and boys and men with sticks marching forward and the rabbits bounding before them in droves; and the swift rush of water in the irrigation canals and the fish panting in the mud where the canals were dry and rotting in the sun where the mud had dried. I had come back to Kansas City and rode the Rock Island and the MK&T through Topeka, Wichita, and Tulsa. It was Oklahoma, Kansas, and Colorado, and no jobs, from spring to fall. Now it was September.

"What will you do in Alabama?" he said.

"Go to school. Work my way."

"And you will study . . . ?"

"Music."

"Very fine. Negroes make fine musicians. We wish you luck, don't we, Mother?" He touched the old woman.

She turned from looking out the door, the distance still in her eyes.

"What is it?" she said.

"He's going to study music. I said we wish him luck, don't we?"

"Oh, yes. Great luck. Won't you have another sandwich? There's plenty."

I took the sandwich. It was very good, and I broke it to save half for Morrie.

"How far have you come?" I asked.

"All the way from Mexia, Texas."

"Never been to Texas," I said. "Lived in Oklahoma all my life, but never got down that far."

"That's too bad. It's a fine country."

I smiled. It was a fine country for *his* kind; mine didn't fare so well there, from what I'd heard.

"If things were as they were a few years ago, I'd invite you down. Our oldest boy had a colored boy for his companion the whole four years he was in school up at Amherst. Fine fellow."

The old lady brightened.

"We have a boy 'bout your age," she said.

"Yes?"

"Yes," the old man said. "He ran away five years ago. We didn't hear hide nor hair of him until six months ago. We're on our way to see him now, at Joplin. It will be a big surprise for him. Five years ago, we would not have had to make the trip in this manner."

"He's at Joplin, Missouri?"

"That's right. He's to be released tomorrow. We haven't seen him for five years. He was a fine boy then. He's still a fine boy," he added hopefully.

I did not know what to say. Joplin was where the Missouri State Reformatory was located.

"I hope you find him well," I said finally.

"Thank you. We are very happy, and very anxious to see him. When we had money, we lost our boy. Now the money is gone, and our boy will be back with us. We are very happy."

"I guess I had better get out and find my buddy," I said. "We'll have to go over to Kentucky to catch the L&N freight going south."

"You must be careful. We need more musicians, like Roland Hayes. You said you sing, didn't you?"

"No," I said. "I play the piano."

"Well, you be careful."

The old lady's face was still bright from the talk of her son.

"Goodbye," I said.

"Goodbye, and be careful."

He handed me a wrapped sandwich. I stuck it in my pocket and climbed out of the car.

When the manifest slowed into the yards at St. Louis, I dropped down into the car and said goodbye again. They were very fine people. I thought of them a few days later when we got into Decatur. The bulls were in the railroad yards as we rolled into town. They came into the cars looking for girls and took me off and threw me into jail. In jail I learned about Scottsboro, and I was glad when Morrie made his way down to Montgomery and got in touch with the school officials, who finally got me out. I thought of the old couple often during those days I lay in jail, and I was sorry that I had not learned their names.

A Hard Time Keeping Up

The train pulled in town at 4 A.M. It had been snowing for thirty miles back, and the warm air in the diner made frost on the glass panes. Snow was piled along the window ledges.

There had been few people in for the last meal, and looking out the car window I had seen five or six rabbits hopping along at leisure in the falling snow. It was very comfortable in the car. The jingle of silver and ice in the pitchers had been very cheerful. When we pulled into the station, we hated to leave the train, but the crew came up to switch the cars, so we decided to grab a trolley across town to the Negro section for a room. Ma Brown's would be swell if she could take us. We walked over to the trolley and waited, but no car came. Overhead the elevated went streaking along, leaving a haze of blue sparks in the white snow.

We stood there watching them sail by.

"Let's grab one of them," I said. "It's faster."

"Yeah but tonight the damn things all go in the wrong direction," Joe said.

"Well, let's get a cab then," I said.

I was getting cold.

"Seem like they're all gone too," Joe said. "No cabs, no trolley, the El going in the wrong direction, and here it is a million below."

"Come on," I said. "Let's get going."

Joe was tall and stoopy, with a friendly grin and eyeglasses and the stride of a walking champ. I had a hard time keeping up. I always had a hard time keeping up with Joe. The snow was falling fast, very fast, and the wind blew some of it down my collar. After everyone had gone in for the night, the snow had filled in the path along where the sidewalk had been.

"Let's get the hell out in the street," Joe said.

"Yeah," I said. "It's easier going."

We walked along where the trolley had cut ruts in the snow. The snow had turned to ice, and under the streetlights the rusting rails made it look like a cigarette stain. The ruts were filling rapidly with the fresh snow. By the time the cars came to carry folks to work, the tracks would be well hidden.

The streetlights and the neon signs made you think of Christmas as they sparkled on the whiteness. It was pleasant to think about the snow, and a piece of red candy some kid dropped had melted into a red frozen stream, reminding me of the first snow I'd seen with blood on it. It was beautiful and sad. We kids had been playing with our new toys and had watched them carry the man away. He was cut and had been there freezing all through the night.

Joe and I passed a cat standing on a door step, howling. His folks had forgotten to let him in for the night, and he sounded like the whole world had gone away to Florida and there was no one left in town but him, the ice, and the snow.

"Listen at that bastard," Joe said.

"He's cold," I said.

"Serves him right. Cats are unlucky as hell."

"Remember the story about 'You Gonna Be Here When Martin Come'?" I said.

"Yeah, girl in Topeka told it to me."

"Women can tell all the dirty stories—worse than men any day."

"Yeah, they sho can."

We passed a corner, and the wind whipped our coattails between our legs. Off somewhere we could hear the elevated rattling along, wheels screeching as it came to a stop. Snow powdered the blue of Joe's coat. There were toys in one of the store windows along the street, and a mouse was building a nest of the stuffing he pulled from a teddy bear. The teddy made no protest as I stopped to watch.

"Come on, damn fool," Joe called.

The wind was from the north, and we had to bend slightly forward as we pushed into the rush of air. Sometimes we turned our backs to the wind.

"It's a killer, boy," I said.

"You ain't no lying chile," Joe said.

"How'd you like to be in Pensacola now?"

"Come on, man, don't start that stuff."

"Think of the sun, and the boats coming up the gulf all clean and white from Nassau and Cuba, and the fish in the blue water, and the long rides around the gulf road at night we used to take with the girls and beer, and the fat guy singing Cuban love songs . . ."

"You think about it. This damn wind won't let me," Joe said. "Besides, there's too many crackers down that way for me."

We were climbing a steep hill, and no cars had been along that way all day. The snow was deep, and when we reached the level stretch at the top it was like walking through high grass after rabbits. A piece of newspaper flew up ahead of us, flopping and crackling in the wind.

"What the hell's this?" Joe said.

I laughed.

An old white fellow popped out of a doorway. He wore no overcoat, and talked with a drawl.

"Would one of you gents . . . ?"

"Now what?" asked Joe.

"Would one of you gents please . . . ?"

"Give him some change."

"I don't have any change."

"Well, give him something and let's get the hell on outa this wind."

I gave the old fellow a bag of sandwiches I'd brought from the diner.

"Thank you, gents," he said. "Thank you very much. Thank you very, very much."

"Yeah," said Joe.

The old fellow looked at him a second, then disappeared

between two buildings. We walked on in the snow. It was quiet now, and the packed snow went *crunch crunch* beneath our feet.

"That guy'll see you tomorrow with two bits in his pocket and call you a black son-uva-bitch," Joe said.

"Oh well," I said.

We had come to where most of the boys used to stop when they were in overnight from a run, and we were glad to get there. Ma Brown ran the place and she cooked the best meals in town. It was like coming home. We put up our bags and walked over across the street to Tom's place to drink Hot Toddies before turning in. Tom's place was an old storefront that he had made into a bar and restaurant and that tended to be dark like Tom. Inside there was a group of fellows standing around the bar, and the nickel phonograph was playing "Summertime." Two fellows were rolling dice on a table in the back of the room, and those at one end of the bar were laughing at some joke. A girl in blue-and-white was drinking Pink Ladies with two fellows at a table. She had nice hands, and a stone sparkled from one of her red-tipped fingers. The fellows were pretty high, and were dressed well. One was a big guy, a hell of a guy. Big as Paul Robeson, with a complexion of a shade that Ma Brown would call "right dark." He was dark as east hell at midnight.

"That boy kinda bring out the color in that gal's cheeks," Joe said.

"She looks like a fay chick."

"Pretty close to the old Mason and Dixon Line for that kind of stuff," Joe said.

"Hell, she's one of us," I said.

"Sure, *we* know it, but do *they* know it?"

"This is not the South, you know."

"So what," Joe said. "Did you you ever hear about the riot they had here?" he said.

"Oh sure, but that was a hell of a time ago," I said.

"Poor little damn fool," Joe said.

He emptied his glass. The drinks were good.

"Aw you long-legged bastard," I said. "Old Joe from the Glory Hole."

The girl and the fellows ordered another round of drinks. They were becoming noisy. She got up from the table and walked around to the big guy's chair and leaned over his back with her arms around his neck. She laughed and her teeth flashed between her red lips. She hollered over to Tom, who was mixing drinks at the bar.

"Tommy! This is my sweet papa Charlie, Tommy," she called. "He's Mama's little boy."

Tom, in his white apron and white teeth, was mixing drinks and laughing with the fellows around the bar. His head, bald and black, shone in the light from the back bar.

The girl rubbed the fellow's head. He grinned and continued to drink. He liked it though, the rubbing and the hugging. She had on a heavy perfume.

"Don't you think he's cute, Tommy?" she called.

Tommy was busy.

"Tommy! Tommy darling! Don't you think my baby's cute?"

"Yeah, babe," laughed Tom. "The blacker the berry the sweeter the juice."

The big guy snuggled up to her like a big cat.

• • •

"Look at that clown," Joe said, pointing at the door.

"He's got something there," I said.

The fellows at the bar broke out with a gale of laughter just as the man entered the brightness of the room. He stood there blinking his eyes at the light and swaying.

"Ain't none of you sons-a-bitches gonna mess wid me or nona my family," he said.

He swayed, looking around the room.

"Nawsuh," he said. "Or nona my goddamn family."

There was white on his knees where he had fallen in the snow.

"Jack's got his correct gauge and is ready," somebody said.

"I mean!" the fellow said, still swaying.

He was gauged all right. The boys failed to challenge him, so he walked over to the bar.

"Don't nobody mess wid me when I'm in my liquor," he said. "My boss mon don't fool with me then."

The others returned to their drinks.

"Come on, let's get over to Ma's," Joe said, "before Big Ike comes in here to collect his cut. He and his boys'll see that little broad and maybe think she's white and start raising hell."

Big Ike controlled all the clubs in the district.

"Ike won't give a damn," I said.

"Come on, Mister Bastard, we're getting the hell out of here."

"Okay. I've had enough anyway."

As we turned to leave the bar, Big Ike and his boys came pushing through the door in a mass. We could smell their liquor as we started past them near the door.

"Don't rush off, boys," Tom called.

"Naw," Joe hollered back. "We're turning in. Had a tough run."

"Well, good night, boys," Tom said.

"Good night, boys," called the girl.

Some of the boys around the bar started to sing "Good Night, Ladies," but one of Ike's crowd put a nickel in the phonograph and they stopped suddenly.

The girl was very lovely as I looked back from the door. All in blue-and-white and the smile still nice in spite of her being high. And when the fellow stood up, they made a fine sight. Even though he staggered, wiping his mouth with the back of one hand and holding on to the back of his chair with the other, his teeth milk-white in his black face, you could not help but see what a swell-looking animal a big bastard could be. Down South they call them "buck niggers," and he was the kind they had kept at stud. As I walked back to Ma's with Joe, I wondered what it was they had done to us. Take a big guy like that; there were plenty of them down South, but they got it in the behind like all the rest. They must have trained something out of us during slavery like they do wildness in a hunting dog. Up to a certain point we had something; then, after that, whatever it is, we didn't have it anymore. One thing, we are all lone wolves, each one trying to fight it out alone—like the guy in Birmingham who stood off a whole police force by himself. Once I'd had a fight with a gang of fay boys myself. I was on my way to the swimming hole and passed the fay boy sitting on an orchard fence.

"Hello, Coon. Coon. Coon! Coon, I bet your name's Rastus," he'd yelled. He was about my size and wore the same

kind of overalls. I walked past him, but he continued to holler, "Coon, coon, look at tha' coon," so I said, "This white peck wants a fight," and I turned and went back. The boy kept on hollering and when I reached him he started to laugh. I was pretty mad by then, and when I came to him, I didn't say a word. I snatched him off the fence and let him have one in the mouth and he yelled . . . Joe and I were back to Ma Brown's by now and were climbing the stairs to our rooms on the second floor. At the turn of the stairs there was a table with a copy of the Singing Boys hanging from the wall. I'd read about them in high school . . . *Anyway this fay kid yelled, "Come on, gang," and rocks started shooting down on my head from the trees, and he reached out and grabbed me.* I was thinking of all this when there was a shot, then four fast ones, coming from somewhere very close to Ma's place.

"That Ike, I bet," said Joe.

"Come on, we can see Tom's place from the window in my room."

"I knew he wouldn't like that big guy and that broad being together," he said.

We ran up the stairs and looked out the window. Down the street we could see Ike and his boys out in front of Tom's. A bullet went zinging up the street, and knocked an insulator off the lamppost in front of Ma's house, and I could hear the *crack crack crack* of the guns. There was about seven of them, all shooting.

Then we saw the big guy. He was headed in our direction and was running like the anchor man on a relay team and when he passed through the circle of light he was naked and there was red on the front of his body, which rippled and shone in the light. Joe had opened the window and when the big fellow passed, taking long clean fast strides, we could see his lips moving like he was counting to himself. It was funny that he could run so smooth after all the drinks. In the snow, with his black skin shining, he looked even bigger than Paul Robeson.

Ike and his boys had quit shooting, and started hollering to raise hell. I started up to say something to Joe, and he was crying and started cussing and wishing for a machine gun. He was shaking like a leaf he was so damn mad.

Then the sirens started up, and Ike and the gang jumped in their cars and beat it. They took the corner on two wheels. Windows started opening, and doors were opening all up the street. Joe hollered for me to come on, and just before I started to leave the window, I looked and saw the big guy turning the corner where Tom's place stood. He was running slow now, and when he got around the corner he fell plunging into the group of fellows standing in the doorway.

I ran to catch up with Joe, because he was mad as hell and might try to clean out the joint single-handed. I stepped into the deep snow and into some slush near the curb where there was a hot pipe that carried steam into the building. God, I thought, the poor guy's all hurt and shot with the liquor and so confused that he doesn't know where he's run to. I caught Joe before he got there, and when we started in, a squad car rolled up with its siren dying away. The cops rushed in and we followed behind.

The big guy was laying up on some tables they'd pulled together in the rear of the room with his shorts on, and the little broad was rubbing him down with something out of a bottle. She was laughing.

The little bitch, I thought. The goddamn lousy little bitch.

Then I looked at Tom, and he was laughing with his belly shaking beneath his clean white apron, and the guys who had been in the door were laughing, and Sam, the waiter coming from the kitchen with a pot of something steaming in his hands, was laughing. Everybody in the place was laughing except Joe and the cops and me. We just stopped still; then I looked at Joe. Joe looked at me. A cop hollered, "What the hell's going on here?" and Joe hollered, "Who shot that man?"

Joe looked as though his eyes would pop out of his head, and little ridges and streams of sweat lined his face. The crowd laughed harder after the cop asked who shot the big guy, and then the cop made a grab for the guy and cooled him with a blackjack. The others fell back but were still laughing some. Then Tom tried to catch his breath and explain to the cops.

"It's all right, boys," he said.

"Yeah, it's all right," someone else said.

Tom was trying hard to get his breath. The cops were not convinced it was all right.

"What in the hell happened?" I said.

The little broad was still pretty high and kept right on laughing.

"Shut that broad's mouth," someone yelled.

"It's all a bet, boys," Tom laughed.

He knocked over a glass as he leaned back on the bar, still trying to catch his breath.

"What kind of a goddamn bet?"

"Just a bet, boy. Ha ha ha."

"Is he hurt bad?" someone who had just come in asked.

"See that, Al, see that? This is your damn Chicago. Here they shoot a man on a bet," Joe yelled.

He was yelling at the top of his voice.

"Ha ha, gawddamn, take it easy, boys. It's just a bet," laughed Tom.

He finally had his breath and started to talk. In the back the big fellow was breathing easier, and the little broad, still laughing, was rubbing him with a towel.

"That Ike's a dog," someone said.

"Nawsuh," someone else said. "Ike don't give a damn 'bout nothing."

"Man, he sho don't, and he likes his sport too."

"You see," Tom said, "Charlie here used to know Mistah Ike when they wuz kids, and when Charlie sees him come in, he remembered him and offered to buy him a drink."

Someone started laughing again.

"That's it," a fellow said.

"Charlie," Tom went on, "wanted Mistah Ike to have a Singapore Sling, but Mistah Ike said that was too sweet and was bad for folks to drink."

"Go on, Tom, let's have it," said a cop.

"Well, Charlie there said Mistah Ike was wrong 'cause sugar is good to give you energy, and he knowed 'cause he's a professional football player and eats candy 'fore every game."

"That sho was funny," someone said.

"Shut up," a cop said.

Tom went on.

"Mistah Ike told Charlie he was lying and looked like he was drunk, and that he ought to cut out the bulling and hanging around with the women folks that early in the morning. So Charlie bet Mistah Ike that he could drink a Sling and run around the block buck-nude without getting cold. Mistah Ike took him on, and told him to get out of his clothes and get going."

"Yeah, yeah, so he runs out and got shot, I guess," the cop said.

"Naw, that war'nt no blood. Miss Flo there just threw some catsup on him when he started out, and them shots was Mistah Ike giving Charlie the signal to go."

"Ain't this a damn shame," someone who had come in late said. The crowd in the door started breaking up, and the cops went to find Big Ike.

"Let's get the hell outa here," Joe said.

When we went out, the lights were going off up along the street and a milk truck was cutting new ruts in the snow. As we walked, I looked at Joe and grinned.

"Aw you ass," he said.

We were both relieved. *I* was very damn much relieved.

The Black Ball

I had rushed through the early part of the day mopping the lobby, placing fresh sand in the tall green jars, sweeping and dusting the halls, and emptying the trash to be burned later on in the day into the incinerator. And I had stopped only once to chase out after a can of milk for Mrs. Johnson, who had a new baby and who was always nice to my boy. I had started at six o'clock, and around eight I ran out to the quarters where we lived over the garage to dress the boy and give him his fruit and cereal. He was very thoughtful sitting there in his high chair and paused several times with his spoon midway to his mouth to watch me as I chewed my toast.

"What's the matter, son?"

"Daddy, am I black?"

"Of course not, you're brown. You know you're not black."

"Well yesterday Jackie said I was so black."

"He was just kidding. You musn't let them kid you, son."

[He was four, a little brown boy in blue rompers, and when he talked and laughed with imaginary playmates, his voice was soft and round in its accents like those of most Negro Americans.]

"Brown's much nicer than white, isn't it, Daddy?"

"Some people think so. But American is better than both, son."

"Is it, Daddy?"

"Sure it is. Now forget this talk about you being black, and Daddy will be back as soon as he finishes his work."

I left him to play with his toys and a book of pictures until I returned. He was a pretty nice fellow, as he used to say after particularly quiet afternoons while I tried to study, and for which quietness he expected a treat of candy or a "picture movie," and I often let him alone while I attended to my duties in the apartments.

I had gone back and started doing the brass on the front doors when a fellow came up and stood watching from the street. He was lean and red in the face with that redness that comes from a long diet of certain foods. You see much of it in the deep South, and here in the Southwest it is not uncommon. He stood there watching, and I could feel his eyes in my back as I polished the brass.

I gave special attention to that brass because for Berry, the manager, the luster of these brass panels and door handles was the measure of all my industry. It was near time for him to arrive.

"Good morning, John," he would say, looking not at me but at the brass.

"Good morning, sir," I would say, looking not at him but at the brass. Usually his face was reflected there. For him, I *was* there. Besides that brass, his money, and the half-dozen or so plants in his office, I don't believe he had any other real interests in life.

There must be no flaws this morning. Two fellows who worked at the building across the street had already been dismissed because whites had demanded their jobs, and with the boy at that age needing special foods and me planning to enter school again next term, I couldn't afford to allow something like that out on the sidewalk to spoil my chances. Especially since Berry had told one of my friends in the building that he didn't like that "damned educated nigger."

I was so concerned with the brass that when the fellow spoke, I jumped with surprise.

"Howdy," he said. The expected drawl was there. But something was missing, something usually behind that kind of drawl.

"Good morning."

"Looks like you working purty hard over that brass."

"It gets pretty dirty overnight."

That part wasn't missing. When they did have something to say to us, they always became familiar.

"You been working here long?" he asked, leaning against the column with his elbow.

"Two months."

I turned my back to him as I worked.

"Any other colored folks working here?"

"I'm the only one," I lied. There were two others. It was none of his business anyway.

"Have much to do?"

"I have enough," I said. Why, I thought, doesn't he go on in and ask for the job? Why bother me? Why tempt me to choke him? Doesn't he know we aren't afraid to fight his kind out this way?

As I turned, picking up the bottle to pour more polish into my rag, he pulled a tobacco sack from the pocket of his old blue coat. I noticed his hands were scarred as though they had been burned.

"Ever smoke Durham?" he asked.

"No thank you," I said.

He laughed.

"Not used to anything like that, are you?"

"Not used to what?"

A little more from this guy and I would see red.

"Fellow like me offering a fellow like you something besides a rope."

I stopped to look at him. He stood there smiling with the sack in his outstretched hand. There were many wrinkles around his eyes, and I had to smile in return. In spite of myself I had to smile.

"Sure you won't smoke some Durham?"

"No thanks," I said.

He was fooled by the smile. A smile couldn't change things between my kind and his.

"I'll admit it ain't much," he said. "But it's a helluva lot different."

I stopped the polishing again to see what it was he was trying to get after.

"But," he said, "I've got something really worth a lot; that is, if you're interested."

"Let's hear it," I said.

Here, I thought, is where he tries to put one over on old "George."

"You see, I come out from the union and we intend to organize all the building-service help in this district. Maybe you been reading 'bout it in the papers?"

"I saw something about it, but what's it to do with me?"

"Well, first place we'll make 'em take some of this work off you. It'll mean shorter hours and higher wages, and better conditions in general."

"What you really mean is that you'll get in here and bounce me out. Unions don't want Negro members."

"You mean *some* unions don't. It used to be that way, but things have changed."

"Listen, fellow. You're wasting your time and mine. Your damn unions are like everything else in the country—for whites only. What ever caused *you* to give a damn about a Negro anyway? Why should *you* try to organize Negroes?"

His face had become a little white.

"See them hands?"

He stretched out his hands.

"Yes," I said, looking not at his hands but at the color draining from his face.

"Well, I got them scars in Macon County, Alabama, for saying a colored friend of mine was somewhere else on a day he was supposed to have raped a woman. He was, too, 'cause I was with him. Me and him was trying to borrow some seed fifty miles away when it happened—if it did happen. They made them scars with a gasoline torch and run me out the county 'cause they said I tried to help a nigger make a white woman out a lie. That same night they lynched him and burned down his house. They did that to him and this to me, and both of us was fifty miles away."

He was looking down at his outstretched hands as he talked.

"God," was all I could say. I felt terrible when I looked closely at his hands for the first time. It must have been hell. The skin was drawn and puckered and looked as though it had been fried. Fried hands.

"Since that time I learned a lot," he said. "I been at this kinda thing. First it was the croppers, and when they got to know me and made it too hot, I quit the country and came to town. First it was in Arkansas and now it's here. And the more I move around, the more I see, and the more I see, the more I work."

He was looking into my face now, his eyes blue in his red skin. He was looking very earnestly. I said nothing. I didn't know what to say to that. Perhaps he was telling the truth; I didn't know. He was smiling again.

"Listen," he said. "Now, don't you go trying to figger it all out right now. There's going to be a series of meetings at this number starting tonight, and I'd like mighty much to see you there. Bring any friends along you want to."

He handed me a card with a number and 8 P.M. sharp written on it. He smiled as I took the card and made as if to shake my hand but turned and walked down the steps to the street. I noticed that he limped as he moved away.

"Good morning, John," Mr. Berry said. I turned, and there he stood; derby, long black coat, stick, nose glasses, and all.

He stood gazing into the brass like the wicked queen into her looking glass in the story which the boy liked so well.

"Good morning, sir," I said.

I should have finished long before.

"Did the man I saw leaving wish to see me, John?"

"Oh no, sir. He only wished to buy old clothes."

Satisfied with my work for the day, he passed inside, and I walked around to the quarters to look after the boy. It was near twelve o'clock.

I found the boy pushing a toy back and forth beneath a chair in the little room which I used for a study.

"Hi, Daddy," he called.

"Hi, son," I called. "What are you doing today?"

"Oh, I'm trucking."

"I thought you had to stand up to truck."

"Not that kind, Daddy, this kind."

He held up the toy.

"Ooh," I said. "*That* kind."

"Aw, Daddy, you're kidding. You always kid, don't you, Daddy?"

"No. When you're bad I don't kid, do I?"

"I guess not."

In fact, he wasn't—only enough to make it unnecessary for me to worry because he wasn't.

The business of trucking soon absorbed him, and I went back to the kitchen to fix his lunch and to warm up the coffee for myself.

The boy had a good appetite, so I didn't have to make him eat. I gave him his food and settled into a chair to study, but my mind wandered away, so I got up and filled a pipe hoping that would help, but it didn't, so I threw the book aside and picked up Malraux's *Man's Fate,* which Mrs. Johnson had given me, and tried to read it as I drank a cup of coffee. I had to give that up also. Those hands were on my brain, and I couldn't forget that fellow.

"Daddy," the boy called softly; it's always softly when I'm busy.

"Yes, son."

"When I grow up I think I'll drive a truck."

"You do?"

"Yes, and then I can wear a lot of buttons on my cap like the men that bring the meat to the grocery. I saw a colored man with some today, Daddy. I looked out the window, and a colored man drove the truck today, and, Daddy, he had two buttons on his cap. I could see 'em plain."

He had stopped his play and was still on his knees, beside the chair in his blue overalls. I closed the book and looked at the boy a long time. I must have looked queer.

"What's the matter, Daddy?" he asked. I explained that I was thinking, and got up and walked over to stand looking out the front window. He was quiet for a while; then he started rolling his truck again.

The only nice feature about the quarters was that they were high up and offered a view in all directions. It was afternoon and the sun was brilliant. Off to the side, a boy and girl were playing tennis in a driveway. Across the street a group of little fellows in bright sunsuits were playing on a long stretch of lawn before a white stone building. Their nurse, dressed completely in white except for her dark glasses, which I saw when she raised her head, sat still as a picture, bent over a book on her knees. As the children played, the wind blew their cries over to where I stood, and as I watched, a flock of pigeons swooped down into the driveway near the stretch of green, only to take flight again wheeling in a mass as another child came skipping up the drive pulling some sort of toy. The children saw him and were running toward him in a group when the nurse looked up and called them back. She called something to the child and pointed back in the direction of the garages where he had just come from. I could see him turn slowly around and drag his toy, some kind of bird that flapped its wings like an eagle, slowly after him. He stopped and pulled a flower from one of the bushes that lined the drive, turning to look hurriedly at the nurse, and then ran back down the drive. The child had been Jackie, the little son of the white gardener who worked across the street.

As I turned away I noticed that my boy had come to stand beside me.

"What you looking at, Daddy?" he said.

"I guess Daddy was just looking out on the world."

Then he asked if he could go out and play with his ball, and since I would soon have to go down myself to water the lawn, I told him it would be all right. But he couldn't find the ball; I would have to find it for him.

"All right now," I told him. "You stay in the back out of everybody's way, and you mustn't ask anyone a lot of questions."

I always warned about the questions, even though it did little good. He ran down the stairs, and soon I could hear the *bump bump bump* of his ball bouncing against the garage doors underneath. But since it didn't make a loud noise, I didn't ask him to stop.

I picked up the book to read again, and must have fallen asleep immediately, for when I came to it was almost time to go water the lawn. When I got downstairs the boy was not there. I called, but no answer. Then I went out into the alley in back of the garages to see if he was playing there. There were three older white boys sitting talking on a pile of old packing cases. They looked uneasy when I came up. I asked if they had seen a little Negro boy, but they said they hadn't. Then I went farther down the alley behind the grocery store where the trucks drove up, and asked one of the fellows working there if he had seen my boy. He said he had been working on the platform all afternoon and that he was sure the boy had not been there. As I started away, the four o'clock whistle blew and I had to go water the lawn. I wondered where the boy could have gone. As I came back up the alley I was becoming alarmed. Then it occurred to me that he might have gone out in front in spite of my warning not to. Of course, that was where he would go, out in front to sit on the grass. I laughed at myself for becoming alarmed and decided not to punish him, even though Berry had given instructions that he was not to be seen out in the front without me. A boy that size will make you do that.

As I came around the building past the tall new evergreens, I could hear the boy crying in just that note no other child has, and when I came completely around I found him standing looking up into a window with tears on his face.

"What is it, son?" I asked. "What happened?"

"My ball, my ball, Daddy. My ball," he cried, looking up at the window.

"Yes, son. But what about the ball?"

"He threw it up in the window."

"Who did? Who threw it, son? Stop crying and tell Daddy about it."

He made an effort to stop, wiping the tears away with the back of his hand.

"A big white boy asked me to throw him my ball an', an' he took it and threw it up in that window and ran," he said, pointing.

I looked up just as Berry appeared at the window. The ball had gone into his private office.

"John, is that your boy?" he snapped.

He was red in the face.

"Yessir, but—"

"Well, he's taken his damned ball and ruined one of my plants."

"Yessir."

"You know he's got no business around here in front, don't you?"

"Yes!"

"Well, if I ever see him around here again, you're going to find yourself behind the black ball. Now get him on round to the back and then come up here and clean up this mess he's made."

I gave him one long hard look and then felt for the boy's hand to take him back to the quarters. I had a hard time seeing as we walked back, and scratched myself by stumbling into the evergreens as we went around the building.

The boy was not crying now, and when I looked down at

him, the pain in my hand caused me to notice that it was bleeding. When we got upstairs, I sat the boy in a chair and went looking for iodine to doctor my hand.

"If anyone should ask me, young man, I'd say your face needed a good washing."

He didn't answer then, but when I came out of the bathroom, he seemed more inclined to talk.

"Daddy, what did that man mean?"

"Mean how, son?"

"About a black ball. You know, Daddy."

"Oh—that."

"You know, Daddy. What'd he mean?"

"He meant, son, that if your ball landed in his office again, Daddy would go after it behind the old black ball."

"Oh," he said, very thoughtful again. Then, after a while he told me: "Daddy, that white man can't see very good, can he, Daddy?"

"Why do you say that, son?"

"Daddy," he said impatiently. "Anybody can see my ball is white."

For the second time that day I looked at him a long time.

"Yes, son," I said. "Your ball *is* white." Mostly white, anyway, I thought.

"Will I play with the black ball, Daddy?"

"In time, son," I said. "In time."

He had already played with the ball; that he would discover later. He was learning the rules of the game already, but he didn't know it. Yes, he would play with the ball. Indeed, poor little rascal, he would play until he grew sick of playing. My, yes, the old ball game. But I'd begin telling him the rules later.

My hand was still burning from the scratch as I dragged the hose out to water the lawn, and looking down at the iodine stain, I thought of the fellow's fried hands, and felt in my pocket to make sure I still had the card he had given me. Maybe there was a color other than white on the old ball.

King of the Bingo Game

The woman in front of him was eating roasted peanuts that smelled so good that he could barely contain his hunger. He could not even sleep and wished they'd hurry and begin the bingo game. There, on his right, two fellows were drinking wine out of a bottle wrapped in a paper bag, and he could hear soft gurgling in the dark. His stomach gave a low, gnawing growl. If this was down South, he thought, all I'd have to do is lean over and say, "Lady, gimme a few of those peanuts, please, ma'm," and she'd pass me the bag and never think nothing of it. Or he could ask the fellows for a drink in the same way. Folks down South stuck together that way; they didn't even have to

From *Tomorrow,* November 1944

know you. But up here it was different. Ask somebody for something, and they'd think you were crazy. Well, I ain't crazy. I'm just broke, 'cause I got no birth certificate to get a job, and Laura 'bout to die 'cause we got no money for a doctor. But I ain't crazy. And yet a pinpoint of doubt was focused in his mind as he glanced toward the screen and saw the hero stealthily entering a dark room and sending the beam of a flashlight along a wall of bookcases. This is where he finds the trapdoor, he remembered. The man would pass abruptly through the wall and find the girl tied to a bed, her legs and arms spread wide, and her clothing torn to rags. He laughed softly to himself. He had seen the picture three times, and this was one of the best scenes.

On his right the fellow whispered wide-eyed to his companion, "Man, look a-yonder!"

"Damn!"

"Wouldn't I like to have her tied up like that . . ."

"Hey! That fool's letting her loose!"

"Aw, man, he loves her."

"Love or no love!"

The man moved impatiently beside him, and he tried to involve himself in the scene. But Laura was on his mind. Tiring quickly of watching the picture, he looked back to where the white beam filtered from the projection room above the balcony. It started small and grew large, specks of dust dancing in its whiteness as it reached the screen. It was strange how the beam always landed right on the screen and didn't mess up and fall somewhere else. But they had it all fixed. Everything was fixed. Now suppose when they showed that girl with her dress torn the girl started taking off the rest of her clothes, and when the guy came in he didn't untie her but kept her there and went to taking off his own clothes? *That* would be something to see. If a picture got out of hand like that those guys up there would go nuts. Yeah, and there'd be so many folks in here you couldn't find a seat for nine months! A strange sensation played over his skin. He shuddered. Yesterday he'd seen a bedbug on a woman's neck as they walked out into the bright street. But exploring his thigh through a hole in his pocket he found only goose pimples and old scars.

The bottle gurgled again. He closed his eyes. Now a dreamy music was accompanying the film and train whistles were sounding in the distance, and he was a boy again walking along a railroad trestle down South, and seeing the train coming, and running back as fast as he could go, and hearing the whistle blowing, and getting off the trestle to solid ground just in time, with the earth trembling beneath his feet, and feeling relieved as he ran down the cinder-strewn embankment onto the highway, and looking back and seeing with terror that the train had left the track and was following him right down the middle of the street, and all the white people laughing as he ran screaming . . .

"Wake up there, buddy! What the hell do you mean hollering like that? Can't you see we trying to enjoy this here picture?"

He stared at the man with gratitude.

"I'm sorry, old man," he said. "I musta been dreaming."

"Well, here, have a drink. And don't be making no noise like that, damn!"

His hands trembled as he tilted his head. It was not wine

but whiskey. Cold rye whiskey. He took a deep swoller, decided it was better not to take another, and handed the bottle back to its owner.

"Thanks, old man," he said.

Now he felt the cold whiskey breaking a warm path straight through the middle of him, growing hotter and sharper as it moved. He had not eaten all day, and it made him light-headed. The smell of the peanuts stabbed him like a knife, and he got up and found a seat in the middle aisle. But no sooner did he sit than he saw a row of intense-faced young girls, and got up again, thinking, You chicks musta been Lindy-hopping somewhere. He found a seat several rows ahead as the lights came on, and he saw the screen disappear behind a heavy red-and-gold curtain; then the curtain rising, and the man with the microphone and a uniformed attendant coming on the stage.

He felt for his bingo cards, smiling. The guy at the door wouldn't like it if he knew about his having *five* cards. Well, not everyone played the bingo game; and even with five cards he didn't have much of a chance. For Laura, though, he had to have faith. He studied the cards, each with its different numerals, punching the free center hole in each and spreading them neatly across his lap; and when the lights faded, he sat slouched in his seat so that he could look from his cards to the bingo wheel with but a quick shifting of his eyes.

Ahead, at the end of the darkness, the man with the microphone was pressing a button attached to a long cord and spinning the bingo wheel and calling out the number each time the wheel came to rest. And each time the voice rang out, his finger raced over the cards for the number. With five cards he had to move fast. He became nervous; there were too many cards, and the man went too fast with his grating voice. Perhaps he should just select one and throw the others away. But he was afraid. He became warm. Wonder how much Laura's doctor would cost? Damn that, watch the cards! And with despair he heard the man call three in a row which he missed on all five cards. This way he'd never win . . .

When he saw the row of holes punched across the third card, he sat paralyzed and heard the man call three more numbers before he stumbled forward, screaming, "Bingo! Bingo!"

"Let that fool up there," someone called.

"Get up there, man!"

He stumbled down the aisle and up the steps to the stage into a light so sharp and bright that for a moment it blinded him, and he felt that he had moved into the spell of some strange, mysterious power. Yet it was as familiar as the sun, and he knew it was the perfectly familiar bingo.

The man with the microphone was saying something to the audience as he held out his card. A cold light flashed from the man's finger as the card left his hand. His knees trembled. The man stepped closer, checking the card against the numbers chalked on the board. Suppose he had made a mistake? The pomade on the man's hair made him feel faint, and he backed away. But the man was checking the card over the microphone now, and he had to stay. He stood tense, listening.

"Under the *O,* forty-four," the man chanted. "Under the *I,* seven. Under the *G,* three. Under the *B,* ninety-six. Under the *N,* thirteen!"

His breath came easier as the man smiled at the audience.

"Yessir, ladies and gentlemen, he's one of the chosen people!"

The audience rippled with laughter and applause.

"Step right up to the front of the stage."

He moved slowly forward, wishing that the light was not so bright.

"To win tonight's jackpot of $36.90 the wheel must stop between the double zero, understand?"

He nodded, knowing the ritual from the many days and nights he had watched the winners march across the stage to press the button that controlled the spinning wheel and receive the prizes. And now he followed the instructions as though he'd crossed the slippery stage a million prize-winning times.

The man was making some kind of a joke, and he nodded vacantly. So tense had he become that he felt a sudden desire to cry, and shook it away. He felt vaguely that his whole life was determined by the bingo wheel; not only that which would happen now that he was at last before it, but all that had gone before, since his birth and his mother's birth and the birth of his father. It had always been there, even though he had not been aware of it, handing out the unlucky cards and numbers of his days. The feeling persisted, and he started quickly away. I better get down from here before I make a fool of myself, he thought.

"Here, boy," the man called. "You haven't started yet."

Someone laughed as he went hesitantly back.

"Are you all reet?"

He grinned at the man's jive talk, but no words would come, and he knew it was not a convincing grin. For suddenly he knew that he stood on the slippery brink of some terrible embarrassment.

"Where are you from, boy?" the man asked.

"Down South."

"He's from down South, ladies and gentlemen," the man said. "Where from? Speak right into the mike."

"Rocky Mont," he said. "Rock' Mont, North Car'lina."

"So you decided to come down off that mountain to the U.S.," the man laughed. He felt that the man was making a fool of him, but then something cold was placed in his hand, and the lights were no longer behind him.

Standing before the wheel he felt alone, but that was somehow right, and he remembered his plan. He would give the wheel a short quick twirl. Just a touch of the button. He had watched it many times, and always it came close to double zero when it was short and quick. He steeled himself; the fear had left, and he felt a profound sense of promise, as though he were about to be repaid for all the things he'd suffered all his life. Trembling, he pressed the button. There was a whirl of lights, and in a second he realized with finality that though he wanted to, he could not stop. It was as though he held a high-powered line in his naked hand. His nerves tightened. As the wheel increased its speed it seemed to draw him more and more into his power, as though it held his fate; and with it came a deep need to submit, to whirl, to lose himself in its swirl of color. He could not stop it now, he knew. So let it be.

The button rested snugly in his palm where the man had placed it. And now he became aware of the man beside him, advising him through the microphone while, behind, the shadowy audience hummed with noisy voices. He shifted his feet. There was still that feeling of helplessness within him, making part of him desire to turn back, even now that the jackpot was right in his hand.

He squeezed the button until his fist ached. Then, like the sudden shriek of a subway whistle, a doubt tore through his head. Suppose he did not spin the wheel long enough? What could he do, and how could he tell? And then he knew, even as he wondered, that as long as he pressed the button, he could control the jackpot. He and only he could determine whether or not it was to be his. Not even the man with the microphone could do anything about it now. He felt drunk. Then, as though he had come down from a high hill into a valley of people, he heard the audience yelling.

"Come down from there, you jerk!"

"Let somebody else have a chance . . ."

"Ole Jack thinks he done found the end of the rainbow . . ."

The last voice was not unfriendly, and he turned and smiled dreamily into the yelling mouths. Then he turned his back squarely on them.

"Don't take too long, boy," a voice said.

He nodded. They were yelling behind him. Those folks did not understand what had happened to him. They had been playing the bingo game day in and night out for years, trying to win rent money or hamburger change. But not one of those wise guys had discovered this wonderful thing. He watched the wheel whirling past the numbers and experienced a burst of exaltation: This is God! This is the really truly God! He said it aloud: "This is God!"

He said it with such absolute conviction that he feared he would fall fainting into the footlights. But the crowd yelled so loud that they could not hear. Those fools, he thought. I'm here trying to tell them the most wonderful secret in the world, and they're yelling like they gone crazy. A hand fell upon his shoulder.

"You'll have to make a choice now, boy. You've taken too long."

He brushed the hand violently away.

"Leave me alone, man. I know what I'm doing!"

The man looked surprised and held on to the microphone for support. And because he did not wish to hurt the man's feelings he smiled, realizing with a sudden pang that there was no way of explaining to the man just why he had to stand there pressing the button forever.

"Come here," he called tiredly.

The man approached, rolling the heavy microphone across the stage.

"Anybody can play this bingo game, right?" he said.

"Sure, but . . ."

He smiled, feeling inclined to be patient with this slick-looking white man with his blue sport shirt and his sharp gabardine suit.

"That's what I thought," he said. "Anybody can win the jackpot as long as they get the lucky number, right?"

"That's the rule, but after all . . ."

"That's what I thought," he said. "And the big prize goes to the man who knows how to win it?"

The man nodded speechlessly.

"Well then, go on over there and watch me win like I want to. I ain't going to hurt nobody," he said, "and I'll show you how to win. I mean to show the whole world how it's got to be done."

And because he understood, he smiled again to let the man know that he held nothing against him for being white and impatient. Then he refused to see the man any longer and stood pressing the button, the voices of the crowd reaching him like sounds in distant streets. Let them yell. All the Negroes down there were just ashamed because he was black like them. He smiled inwardly, knowing how it was. Most of the time he was ashamed of what Negroes did himself. Well, let them be ashamed for something this time. Like him. He was like a long thin black wire that was being stretched and wound upon the bingo wheel; wound until he wanted to scream; wound, but this time himself controlling the winding and the sadness and the shame, and because he did, Laura would be all right. Suddenly the lights flickered. He staggered backward. Had something gone wrong? All this noise. Didn't they know that although he controlled the wheel, it also controlled him, and unless he pressed the button forever and forever and ever it would stop, leaving him high and dry, dry and high on this hard high slippery hill and Laura dead? There was only one chance; he had to do whatever the wheel demanded. And gripping the button in despair, he discovered with surprise that it imparted a nervous energy. His spine tingled. He felt a certain power.

Now he faced the raging crowd with defiance, its screams penetrating his eardrums like trumpets shrieking from a jukebox. The vague faces glowing in the bingo lights gave him a sense of himself that he had never known before. He was running the show, by God! They had to react to him, for he was their luck. This is *me,* he thought. Let the bastards yell. Then someone was laughing inside him, and he realized that somehow he had forgotten his own name. It was a sad, lost feeling to lose your name, and a crazy thing to do. That name had been given him by the white man who had owned his grandfather a long lost time ago down South. But maybe those wise guys knew his name.

"Who am I?" he screamed.

"Hurry up and bingo, you jerk!"

They didn't know either, he thought sadly. They didn't even know their own names, they were all poor nameless bastards. Well, he didn't need that old name; he was reborn. For as long as he pressed the button he was The-man-who-pressed-the-button-who-held-the-prize-who-was-the-King-of-Bingo. That was the way it was, and he'd have to press the button even if nobody understood, even though Laura did not understand.

"Live!" he shouted.

The audience quieted like the dying of a huge fan.

"Live, Laura, baby. I got holt of it now, sugar. Live!"

He screamed it, tears streaming down his face. "I got nobody but YOU!"

The screams tore from his very guts. He felt as though the rush of blood to his head would burst out in baseball seams of small red droplets, like a head beaten by police clubs. Bending over he saw a trickle of blood splashing the toe of his shoe. With his free hand he searched his head. It was his nose. God, suppose something has gone wrong? He felt that the whole audience had somehow entered him and was stamping its feet in his stomach and he was unable to throw them out. They wanted the prize, that was it. They wanted the secret for themselves. But they'd never get it; he would keep the bingo wheel whirling forever, and Laura would be safe in the wheel. But would she? It had to be, because if she were not safe the wheel would cease to turn; it could not go on. He had to get away, *vomit* all, and his mind formed an image of himself running with Laura in his arms down the tracks of the subway just ahead of an A train, running desperately *vomit* with people screaming for him to come out but knowing no way of leaving the tracks because to stop would bring the train crushing down upon him and to attempt to leave across the other tracks would mean to run into a hot third rail as high as his waist which threw blue sparks that blinded his eyes until he could hardly see.

He heard singing, and the audience was clapping its hands.

> *"Shoot the liquor to him, Jim, boy!*
> *Clap-clap-clap*
> *Well a-calla the cop*
> *He's blowing his top!*
> *Shoot the liquor to him, Jim, boy!"*

Bitter anger grew within him at the singing. They think I'm crazy. Well let 'em laugh. I'll do what I got to do.

He was standing in an attitude of intense listening when he saw that they were watching something on the stage behind him. He felt weak. But when he turned he saw no one. If only his thumb did not ache so. Now they were applauding. And for a moment he thought that the wheel had stopped. But that was impossible, his thumb still pressed the button. Then he saw them. Two men in uniform beckoned from the end of the stage. They were coming toward him, walking in step, slowly, like a tap-dance team returning for a third encore. But their shoulders shot forward, and he backed away, looking wildly about. There was nothing to fight them with. He had only the long black cord which led to a plug somewhere backstage, and he couldn't use that because it operated the bingo wheel. He backed slowly, fixing the men with his eyes as his lips stretched over his teeth in a tight, fixed grin; moved toward the end of the stage and realizing that he couldn't go much further, for suddenly the cord became taut and he couldn't afford to break the cord. But he had to do something. The audience was howling. Suddenly he stopped dead, seeing the men halt, their legs lifted as in an interrupted step of a slow-motion dance. There was nothing to do but run in the other direction and he dashed forward, slipping and sliding. The men fell back, surprised. He struck out violently going past.

"Grab him!"

He ran, but all too quickly the cord tightened, resistingly, and he turned and ran back again. This time he slipped them, and discovered by running in a circle before the wheel he could keep the cord from tightening. But this way he had to flail his arms to keep the men away. Why couldn't they leave a man alone? He ran, circling.

"Ring down the curtain," someone yelled. But they couldn't do that. If they did, the wheel flashing from the projection room would be cut off. But they had him before he could tell them so, trying to pry open his fist, and he was wrestling and trying to bring his knees into the fight and holding on to the button, for it was his life. And now he was down, seeing a foot coming down, crushing his wrist cruelly, down, as he saw the wheel whirling serenely above.

"I can't give it up," he screamed. Then quietly, in a confidential tone, "Boys, I really can't give it up."

It landed hard against his head. And in the blank moment they had it away from him, completely now. He fought them trying to pull him up from the stage as he watched the wheel spin slowly to a stop. Without surprise he saw it rest at double zero.

"You see." He pointed bitterly.

"Sure, boy, sure, it's okay," one of the men said, smiling. And seeing the man bow his head to someone he could not see, he felt very, very happy; he would receive what all the winners received.

But as he warmed in the justice of the man's tight smile he did not see the man's slow wink, nor see the bowlegged man behind him step clear of the swiftly descending curtain and set himself for a blow. He only felt the dull pain exploding in his skull, and he knew even as it slipped out of him that his luck had run out on the stage.

In a Strange Country

In the pub his eye had begun to close. White spots danced before him, and he had to cover the eye with his hand in order to see Mr. Catti. Mr. Catti was drinking now, and as the bottom of the glass swung down and tapped the table, he looked into Mr. Catti's pale, sharp-nosed face and smiled. Mr. Catti had been very kind, and he was trying hard to be pleasant.

"You miss this on a ship," he said, draining his glass.

"Do you like our Welsh ale?"

"Very much."

"It's not so good as before the war," Mr. Catti said sadly.

"It must have been very good," he said.

From *Tomorrow,* July 1944

He looked guardedly at the pretty, blue-aproned barmaid, seeing her dark hair shift lazily forward as she drew beer from a pump such as he'd seen only in English pictures. With his eye covered he saw much better. Across the room, near the fireplace with its grate of glowing coals, two men were seeing who could knock over a set of skittlepins. One of them started singing "Treat Me Like an Irish Soldier" as Mr. Catti said:

"Have you been long in Wales?"

"About forty-five minutes," he said.

"Then you have much to see," Mr. Catti said, getting up and carrying the glasses over to the bar to be refilled.

No, he thought, looking at the GUINNESS IS GOOD FOR YOU signs, I've seen enough. Coming ashore from the ship he had felt the excited expectancy of entering a strange land. Moving along the road in the dark he had planned to stay ashore all night, and in the morning he would see the country with fresh eyes, like those with which the Pilgrims had seen the New World. That hadn't seemed so silly then—not until the soldiers bunched at the curb had seemed to spring out of the darkness. Someone had cried, "Jesus H. Christ," and he had thought, He's from home, and grinned and apologized into the light they flashed in his eyes. He had felt the blow coming when they yelled, "It's a goddamn nigger," but it struck him anyway. He was having a time of it when some of Mr. Catti's countrymen stepped in and Mr. Catti had guided him into the pub. Now, over several rounds of ale, they had introduced themselves, had discreetly avoided mentioning his eye, and, while he heard with forced attention something of Welsh national history, he had been adjusting himself to the men in cloth caps and narrow-brimmed hats who talked so quietly over their drinks.

At first he had included them in his blind rage. But they had seemed so genuinely and uncondescendingly polite that he was disarmed. Now the anger and resentment had slowly ebbed, and he felt only a smoldering sense of self-hate and ineffectiveness. Why should he blame them when they had only helped him? *He* had been the one so glad to hear an American voice. You can't take it out on them, they're a different breed; even from the English. That's what he's been telling you, he thought, seeing Mr. Catti returning, his head held to one side to avoid the smoke from his cigarette, the foam-headed glasses caged in his fingers.

"It's a disgrace to our country, Mr. Parker!" Mr. Catti said heatedly. "How is your eye?"

"It's better, thanks," he said, brightening. "And don't worry, it's a sort of family quarrel. Are there many like me in Wales?"

"Oh yes! Yanks all over the place. Black Yanks and white."

"Black *Yanks*?" He wanted to smile.

"Yes. And many a fine lad at that."

Mr. Catti was looking at his wristwatch.

"My, my! I'm sorry, but it's time for my concert. Perhaps you would like to come? The boys at my club are singing—no professionals, mind you, but some very fine voices."

"No . . . no, I'd better not," he said. Yet all music was a passion with him, and his interest was aroused.

"It's a private club," Mr. Catti said reassuringly. "Open only to members—and to our guests, of course. We'd be very glad to have you. Perhaps the boys will sing some of your spirituals."

"Oh! So you know our music, too?"

"Very well," Mr. Catti said. "And since your boys have been with us we've learned that, like ourselves, your people love music."

"I think I'd like very much to go," he said, rising and getting into his seaman's topcoat. "You might have to guide me along though."

"Righto. It isn't far. Just a bit up Straight Street."

Outside, the pale beam of a flashlight revealed the stone walk. Somewhere in the damp darkness a group of adolescent girls were singing a nostalgic Tin Pan Alley tune. Here you go again, he thought. Better go back to the ship, no telling what'll jump out of the darkness next; maybe the Second Avenue El. And suppose someone else brings a Yank? Why spoil the fun? Hell, so let *him* walk out. . . .

Mr. Catti was guiding him into a doorway toward a soft murmur of voices. Maybe, he thought, you'll hear that old "spiritual" classic *Massa's in de—Massa's in de Old Cold Masochism!*

When the light struck his injured eye, it was as though it were being peeled by an invisible hand. He did not know whether to cover it or to let it be so as not to attract attention. What was the use?

Mr. Catti was greeting the men who made room for them at the bar. Looking across the room, where folding chairs were grouped neatly around rows of small tables, he heard a man in a blue suit running brilliant arpeggios upon an upright piano. It was a cheerful room.

"Two whiskeys, Alf," said Mr. Catti to the man behind the bar.

"Right! And a good evening to you, Twm," the man said.

"This is Mr. Parker, Alf," Mr. Catti said, introducing him. "Mr. Parker, Mr. Triffit, our club manager."

"How do you do?" he said, shaking Mr. Triffit's hand.

"Welcome to our club, sir," Mr. Triffit said. "You are an American, I take it?"

"Yes," he said. And with sly amusement he added, "A black Yank."

"I thought Mr. Parker would like the concert, Alf. So I brought him along."

"We're happy to have you, sir," Mr. Triffit said. "I believe you will enjoy it, Mr. Parker. If I do say so myself, our boys are . . . are . . . yes, dammit, they're smashing!"

"I'm sure they are," he said, thinking, He acts like he'd fight over it.

"Here's all the best," said Mr. Catti.

"Your health, sir," said Mr. Triffit.

"To Wales," Mr. Parker said, "and to you both."

"And to America, God bless her," Mr. Triffit said.

"Yes," said Mr. Parker, "and to America."

He could see Mr. Triffit about to mention his eye, and was glad Mr. Catti was moving away.

"Come, Mr. Parker. We'd better select our seats."

They sat near the front, where the singers were grouping themselves to begin. The warmth of the liquor was spreading slowly through him now, and it was with a growing sense of remoteness that he heard the first number announced, a Welsh song to be rendered a cappella. The quiet tuning chord sounded far away. He saw the men set themselves and the conductor raising his hand, then, at the downbeat, the quick, audible intake of breath and the precise attack.

The well-blended voices caught him unprepared. He heard the music's warm richness with pleasurable surprise, and heard, beneath the strange Welsh words, echoes of plain song, like that of Russian folk songs sounding.

"It's wonderful," he whispered, seeing Mr. Catti smile knowingly.

He looked about him. He saw the faces of the listeners caught in a single spell of communication while they sipped their drinks or puffed their pipes or cigarettes. Slowly the hall was filling with friendly swirls of smoke. They were singing another of their songs now, and though he could not understand the words he felt himself drawn closer to its web of meaning. Then the familiar and hateful emotion of alienation gripped his throat.

"It was a song about Wales?" he asked, soothing his eye.

"Exactly!" exclaimed Mr. Catti. "And the other was about a battle in which we defeated the English. Nothing like music to reveal what's in the heart. You don't need lyrics, really."

A warm flush dyed Mr. Catti's face. He's pleased that I understood, he thought. And as the men sang in hushed tones he felt a growing poverty of spirit. He should have known more of the Welsh, of their history and art. If we only had some of what they have, he thought. They are a much smaller nation than ours would be, yet I can remember no song of ours that's of love of the soil or of country. Nor any song of battle other than those of biblical times. And in his mind's eye he saw a Russian peasant kneeling to kiss the earth and rising wet-eyed to enter into battle with cries of fierce exultation. And he felt now, among these men, hearing their voices, a surge of deep longing to know the anguish and exultation of such love.

"Do you see that fellow with the red face there?" asked Mr. Catti.

"Yes."

"Our leading mine owner."

"And what are the others?"

"Everything. The tenor on the end is a miner. Mr. Jones, in the center there, is a butcher. And the dark man next to him is a union official."

"You'd never think so from their harmony," he said, smiling.

"When we sing, we are Welshmen," Mr. Catti said as the next number began.

Parker smiled, aware suddenly of an expansiveness that he had known before only at mixed jam sessions. When we jam, sir, we're Jamocrats! He liked these Welsh. Not even on the ship, where the common danger and a fighting union made for a degree of understanding, did he approach white men so closely.

For that's a unity of economics, he said to himself. And this a unity of music, a "gut language," the "food of love." Go on, fool. Behind that blacked-out eye you can get away with it. Knock yourself out. *All right, I will: Dear Wales, I salute thee. I kiss the lips of thy proud spirit through the fair sounds of thy songs. How's that?* Fine. Slightly mixed in metaphor, but not bad. Give us some more, Othello. *Othello? Indeed, and how odd. But. So: Oh my fair warrior nation, because of thee this little while my chaos is gone again*—Again? Parker, keep to the facts. And remember what they did to Othello. *No, he did it to himself. Couldn't believe in his woman, nor in himself.* I know, so that makes Iago a Fifth Columnist. But what do *you* believe in? *Oh, shut—I believe in music!* Well! *And in what's happening here tonight. I believe . . . I want to believe in this people.* Something was getting out of control. He became on guard. At home he could drown his humanity in a sea of concealed cynicism, and white men would never recognize it. But these men might understand. Perhaps, he felt with vague terror, all evening he had been exposed, blinded by the brilliant light of their deeper humanity, and they had seen him for what he was and for what he should have been. He was sobered. Listening now, he thought, You live on the ship, remember. Down Straight Street, in the dark. And at home you live in Harlem. Quit letting their liquor throw you, or even their hospitality. Do the State some service, Parker. They won't know it. And if these men should, it doesn't matter. Put out that light, Othello—or do you enjoy being hit with one?

"How is your eye now?" Mr. Catti asked.

"Almost completely closed."

"It's a bloody shame!"

"It's been a wonderful evening though," he said. "One of the best I've ever spent."

"I'm glad you came," Mr. Catti said. "And so are the boys. They can tell that you appreciate the music, and they're pleased."

"Here's to singing," he toasted.

"To singing," said Mr. Catti.

"By the way, let me lend you my torch to find your way back. Just return it to Heath's Bookstore. Anyone will direct you."

"But you'll need it yourself."

Mr. Catti placed the light upon the table. "Don't worry," he said. "I'm at home. I know the city like my own palm."

"Thanks," he said with feeling. "You're very kind."

When the opening bars were struck, he saw the others pushing back their chairs and standing, and he stood, understanding even as Mr. Catti whispered, "Our national anthem."

There was something in the music and in the way they held their heads that was strangely moving. He hummed beneath his breath. When it was over he would ask for the words.

But even while he heard the final triumphal chord still sounding, the piano struck up "God Save the King." It was not nearly so stirring. Then swiftly modulating they swept into the "Internationale," to words about an international army. He was carried back to when he was a small boy marching in the streets behind the bands that came to his southern town. . . .

Mr. Catti had nudged him. He looked up, seeing the conductor looking straight at him, smiling. They were all looking at him. Why, was it his eye? Were they playing a joke? And suddenly he recognized the melody and felt that his knees would give way. It was as though he had been pushed into the horrible foreboding country of dreams and they were enticing him into some unwilled and degrading act, from which only his failure to remember the words would save him. It was all unreal, yet it seemed to have happened before. Only now the melody seemed charged with some vast new meaning which that part of him that wanted to sing could not fit with the old familiar words. And beyond the music he kept hearing the soldiers' voices, yelling as they had when the light struck his eye. He saw the singers still staring, and as though to betray him he heard his own voice singing out like a suddenly amplified radio:

> ". . . *Gave proof through the night*
> *That our flag was still there* . . ."

It was like the voice of another, over whom he had no control. His eye throbbed. A wave of guilt shook him, followed by a burst of relief. For the first time in your whole life, he thought with dreamlike wonder, the words are not ironic. He stood in confusion as the song ended, staring into the men's Welsh faces, not knowing whether to curse them or to return their good-natured smiles. Then the conductor was before him, and Mr. Catti was saying, "You're not such a bad singer yourself, Mr. Parker. Is he now, Mr. Morcan?"

"Why, if he'd stay in Wales, I wouldn't rest until he joined the club," Mr. Morcan said. "What about it, Mr. Parker?"

But Mr. Parker could not reply. He held Mr. Catti's flashlight like a club and hoped his black eye would hold back the tears.

Flying Home

When Todd came to, he saw two faces suspended above him in a sun so hot and blinding that he could not tell if they were black or white. He stirred, feeling a pain that burned as though his whole body had been laid open to the sun, which glared into his eyes. For a moment an old fear of being touched by white hands seized him. Then the very sharpness of the pain began slowly to clear his head. Sounds came to him dimly. *He done come to.* Who are they? he thought. *Naw he ain't, I coulda sworn he was white.* Then he heard clearly:

"You hurt bad?"

Something within him uncoiled. It was a Negro sound.

From *Cross Section,* 1944

"He's still out," he heard.

"Give 'im time. . . . Say, son, you hurt bad?"

Was he? There was that awful pain. He lay rigid, hearing their breathing and trying to weave a meaning between them and his being stretched painfully upon the ground. He watched them warily, his mind traveling back over a painful distance. Jagged scenes, swiftly unfolding as in a movie trailer, reeled through his mind, and he saw himself piloting a tailspinning plane and landing and falling from the cockpit and trying to stand. Then, as in a great silence, he remembered the sound of crunching bone and, now, looking up into the anxious faces of an old Negro man and a boy from where he lay in the same field, the memory sickened him and he wanted to remember no more.

"How you feel, son?"

Todd hesitated, as though to answer would be to admit an unacceptable weakness. Then, "It's my ankle," he said.

"Which one?"

"The left."

With a sense of remoteness he watched the old man bend and remove his boot, feeling the pressure ease.

"That any better?"

"A lot. Thank you."

He had the sensation of discussing someone else, that his concern was with some far more important thing, which for some reason escaped him.

"You done broke it bad," the old man said. "We have to get you to a doctor."

He felt that he had been thrown into a tailspin. He looked at his watch; how long had he been here? He knew there was but one important thing in the world, to get the plane back to the field before his officers were displeased.

"Help me up," he said. "Into the ship."

"But it's broke too bad . . ."

"Give me your arm!"

"But, son . . ."

Clutching the old man's arm, he pulled himself up, keeping his left leg clear, thinking, I'd never make him understand, as the leather-smooth face came parallel with his own.

"Now, let's see."

He pushed the old man back, hearing a bird's insistent shrill. He swayed, giddily. Blackness washed over him, like infinity.

"You best sit down."

"No, I'm okay."

"But, son. You jus gonna make it worse . . ."

It was a fact that everything in him cried out to deny, even against the flaming pain in his ankle. He would have to try again.

"You mess with that ankle they have to cut your foot off," he heard.

Holding his breath, he started up again. It pained so badly that he had to bite his lips to keep from crying out and he allowed them to help him down with a pang of despair.

"It's best you take it easy. We gon git you a doctor."

Of all the luck, he thought. Of all the rotten luck, now I have done it. The fumes of high-octane gasoline clung in the heat, taunting him.

"We kin ride him into town on old Ned," the boy said.

Ned? He turned, seeing the boy point toward an ox team, browsing where the buried blade of a plow marked the end of a furrow. Thoughts of himself riding an ox through the town, past streets full of white faces, down the concrete runways of the airfield, made swift images of humiliation in his mind. With a pang he remembered his girl's last letter. "Todd," she had written, "I don't need the papers to tell me you had the intelligence to fly. And I have always known you to be as brave as anyone else. The papers annoy me. Don't you be contented to prove over and over again that you're brave or skillful just because you're black, Todd. I think they keep beating that dead horse because they don't want to say why you boys are not yet fighting. I'm really disappointed, Todd. Anyone with brains can learn to fly, but then what. What about using it, and who will you use it for? I wish, dear, you'd write about this. I sometimes think they're playing a trick on us. It's very humiliating. . . ." He whipped cold sweat from his face, thinking, What does she know of humiliation? She's never been down South. *Now* the humiliation would come. When you must have them judge you, knowing that they never accept your mistakes as your own but hold it against your whole race—that was humiliation. Yes, and humiliation was when you could never be simply yourself; when you were always a part of this old black ignorant man. Sure, he's all right. Nice and kind and helpful. But he's not you. Well, there's one humiliation I can spare myself.

"No," he said. "I have orders not to leave the ship. . . ."

"Aw," the old man said. Then turning to the boy, "Teddy, then you better hustle down to Mister Graves and get him to come. . . ."

"No, wait!" he protested before he was fully aware. Graves might be white. "Just have him get word to the field, please. They'll take care of the rest."

He saw the boy leave, running.

"How far does he have to go?"

"Might' nigh a mile."

He rested back, looking at the dusty face of his watch. By now they know something has happened, he thought. In the ship there was a perfectly good radio, but it was useless. The old fellow would never operate it. That buzzard knocked me back a hundred years, he thought. Irony danced within him like the gnats circling the old man's head. With all I've learned, I'm dependent upon this "peasant's" sense of time and space. His leg throbbed. In the plane, instead of time being measured by the rhythms of pain and a kid's legs, the instruments would have told him at a glance. Twisting upon his elbows, he saw where dust had powdered the plane's fuselage, feeling the lump form in his throat that was always there when he thought of flight. It's crouched there, he thought, like the abandoned shell of a locust. I'm naked without it. Not a machine, a suit of clothes you wear. And with a sudden embarrassment and wonder he whispered, "It's the only dignity I have. . . ."

He saw the old man watching, his torn overalls clinging limply to him in the heat. He felt a sharp need to tell the old man what he felt. But that would be meaningless. If I tried to explain why I need to fly back, he'd think I was simply afraid of white officers. But it's more than fear . . . a sense of anguish clung to him like the veil of sweat that hugged his face. He watched the old man, hearing him humming snatches of a tune as he admired the plane. He felt a furtive sense of resentment. Such old men often came to the field to watch the pilots with childish eyes. At first it had made him proud; they had been a meaningful part of a new experience. But soon he realized they did not understand his accomplishments and they came to shame and embarrass him, like the distasteful praise of an idiot. A part of the meaning of flying had gone, then, and he had not been able to regain it. If I were a prize-fighter I would be more human, he thought. Not a monkey doing tricks, but a man. They were pleased simply that he was a Negro who could fly, and that was not enough. He felt cut off from them by age, by understanding, by sensibility, by technology, and by his need to measure himself against the mirror of other men's appreciation. Somehow he felt betrayed, as he had when as a child he grew to discover that his father was dead. Now, for him, any real appreciation lay with his white officers; and with them he could never be sure. Between ignorant black men and condescending whites, his course of flight seemed mapped by the nature of things away from all needed and natural landmarks. Under some sealed orders, couched in ever more technical and mysterious terms, his path curved swiftly away from both the shame the old man symbolized and the cloudy terrain of white man's regard. Flying blind, he knew but one point of landing and there he would receive his wings. After that the enemy would appreciate his skill and he would assume his deepest meaning, he thought sadly, neither from those who condescended nor from those who praised without understanding, but from the enemy who would recognize his manhood and skill in terms of hate. . . .

He sighed, seeing the oxen making queer, prehistoric shadows against the dry brown earth.

"You just take it easy, son," the old man soothed. "That boy won't take long. Crazy as he is about airplanes."

"I can wait," he said.

"What kinda airplane you call this here'n?"

"An Advanced Trainer," he said, seeing the old man smile. His fingers were like gnarled dark wood against the metal as he touched the low-slung wing.

" 'Bout how fast can she fly?"

"Over two hundred an hour."

"Lawd! That's so fast I bet it don't seem like you moving!"

Holding himself rigid, Todd opened his flying suit. The shade had gone and he lay in a ball of fire.

"You mind if I take a look inside? I was always curious to see . . ."

"Help yourself. Just don't touch anything."

He heard him climb upon the metal wing, grunting. Now the questions would start. Well, so you don't have to think to answer. . . .

He saw the old man looking over into the cockpit, his eyes bright as a child's.

"You must have to know a lot to work all these here things."

Todd was silent, seeing him step down and kneel beside him.

"Son, how come you want to fly way up there in the air?"

Because it's the most meaningful act in the world . . . because it makes me less like you, he thought.

But he said: "Because I like it, I guess. It's as good a way to fight and die as I know."

"Yeah? I guess you right," the old man said. "But how long you think before they gonna let you all fight?"

He tensed. This was the question all Negroes asked, put with the same timid hopefulness and longing that always opened a greater void within him than that he had felt beneath the plane the first time he had flown. He felt lightheaded. It came to him suddenly that there was something sinister about the conversation, that he was flying unwillingly into unsafe and uncharted regions. If he could only be insulting and tell this old man who was trying to help him to shut up!

"I bet you one thing . . ."

"Yes?"

"That you was plenty scared coming down."

He did not answer. Like a dog on a trail the old man seemed to smell out his fears, and he felt anger bubble within him.

"You sho scared *me.* When I seen you coming down in that thing with it a-rollin' and a-jumpin' like a pitchin' hoss, I thought sho you was a goner. I almost had me a stroke!"

He saw the old man grinning. "Ever'thin's been happening round here this morning, come to think of it."

"Like what?" he asked.

"Well, first thing I know, here come two white fellers looking for Mister Rudolph, that's Mister Graves' cousin. That got me worked up right away. . . ."

"Why?"

"Why? 'Cause he done broke outa the crazy house, that's why. He liable to kill somebody," he said. "They oughta have him by now though. Then here *you* come. First I think it's one of them white boys. Then doggone if you don't fall outa there. Lawd, I'd done heard about you boys but I haven't never *seen* one o' you all. Caint tell you how it felt to see somebody what look like me in a airplane!"

The old man talked on, the sound streaming around

Todd's thoughts like air flowing over the fuselage of a flying plane. You were a fool, he thought, remembering how before the spin the sun had blazed, bright against the billboard signs beyond the town, and how a boy's blue kite had bloomed beneath him, tugging gently in the wind like a strange, odd-shaped flower. He had once flown such kites himself and tried to find the boy at the end of the invisible cord. But he had been flying too high and too fast. He had climbed steeply away in exultation. Too steeply, he thought. And one of the first rules you learn is that if the angle of thrust is too steep the plane goes into a spin. And then, instead of pulling out of it and going into a dive you let a buzzard panic you. A lousy buzzard!

"Son, what made all that blood on the glass?"

"A buzzard," he said, remembering how the blood and feathers had sprayed back against the hatch. It had been as though he had flown into a storm of blood and blackness.

"Well, I declare! They's lots of 'em around here. They after dead things. Don't eat nothing what's alive."

"A little bit more and he would have made a meal out of me," Todd said grimly.

"They had luck all right. Teddy's got a name for 'em, calls 'em jimcrows," the old man laughed.

"It's a damned good name."

"They the damnedest birds. Once I seen a hoss all stretched out like he was sick, you know. So I hollers, 'Gid up from there, suh!' Just to make sho! An', doggone, son, if I don't see two old jimcrows come flying right up outa that hoss's insides! Yessuh! The sun was shinin' on 'em and they couldn'ta been no greasier if they'd been eating barbecue!"

Todd thought he would vomit; his stomach quivered.

"You made that up," he said.

"Nawsuh! Saw him just like you."

"Well, I'm glad it was you."

"You see lots a funny things down here, son."

"No, I'll let you see them," he said.

"By the way, the white folks round here don't like to see you boys up there in the sky. They ever bother you?"

"No."

"Well, they'd like to."

"Someone always wants to bother someone else," Todd said. "How do you know?"

"I just know."

"Well," he said defensively, "no one has bothered us."

Blood pounded in his ears as he looked away into space. He tensed, seeing a black spot in the sky, and strained to confirm what he could not clearly see.

"What does that look like to you?" he asked excitedly.

"Just another bad luck, son."

Then he saw the movement of wings with disappointment. It was gliding smoothly down, wings outspread, tail feathers gripping the air, down swiftly—gone behind the green screen of trees. It was like a bird he had imagined there, only the sloping branches of the pines remained, sharp against the pale stretch of sky. He lay barely breathing and stared at the point where it had disappeared, caught in a spell of loathing and admiration. Why did they make them so disgusting and yet teach them to fly so well? *It's like when I was up in heaven,* he heard, starting.

The old man was chuckling, rubbing his stubbled chin.

"What did you say?"

"Sho, I died and went to heaven . . . maybe by time I tell you about it they be done come after you."

"I hope so," he said wearily.

"You boys ever sit around and swap lies?"

"Not often. Is this going to be one?"

"Well, I ain't so sho, on account of it took place when I was dead."

The old man paused. "That wasn't no lie 'bout the buzzards though."

"All right," he said.

"Sho you want to hear 'bout heaven?"

"Please," he answered, resting his head upon his arm.

"Well, I went to heaven and right away started to sproutin' me some wings. Six-foot ones, they was. Just like them the white angels had. I couldn't hardly believe it. I was so glad that I went off on some clouds by myself and tried 'em out. You know, 'cause I didn't want to make a fool outa myself the first thing . . ."

It's an old tale, Todd thought. Told me years ago. Had forgotten. But at least it will keep him from talking about buzzards.

He closed his eyes, listening.

". . . First thing I done was to git up on a low cloud and jump off. And doggone, boy, if them wings didn't work! First I tried the right; then I tried the left; then I tried 'em both together. Then, Lawd, I started to move on out among the folks. I let 'em see me . . ."

He saw the old man gesturing flight with his arms, his face full of mock pride as he indicated an imaginary crowd, thinking, *It'll be in the newspapers,* as he heard, ". . . so I went and found me some colored angels—somehow I didn't believe I was an angel till I seen a real black one, ha, yes! Then I was sho—but they tole me I better come down 'cause us colored folks had to wear a special kin'a harness when we flew. That was how come *they* wasn't flyin'. Oh yes, an' you had to be extra strong for a black man even, to fly with one of them harnesses . . ."

This is a new turn, Todd thought. What's he driving at?

"So I said to myself, I ain't gonna be bothered with no harness! Oh naw! 'Cause if God let you sprout wings you oughta have sense enough not to let nobody make you wear something what gits in the way of flyin'. So I starts to flyin'. Hecks, son," he chuckled, his eyes twinkling, "you know I had to let eve'body know that old Jefferson could fly good as anybody else. And I could too, fly smooth as a bird! I could even loop-the-loop—only I had to make sho to keep my long white robe down roun' my ankles . . ."

Todd felt uneasy. He wanted to laugh at the joke, but his body refused, as of an independent will. He felt as he had as a child when after he had chewed a sugar-coated pill which his mother had given him, she had laughed at his efforts to remove the terrible taste.

". . . Well," he heard. "I was doing all right till I got to speeding. Found out I could fan up a right strong breeze, I could fly so fast. I could do all kin'sa stunts too. I started flying up to the stars and divin' down and zooming roun' the moon. Man, I like to scare the devil outa some ole white angels. I was raisin' hell. Not that I meant any harm, son. But I was just feeling good. It was so good to know I was free at last. I accidentally knocked the tips offa some stars and they tell me I caused a storm and a coupla lynchings down here in Macon County—though I swear I believe them boys what said that was making up lies on me . . ."

He's mocking me, Todd thought angrily. He thinks it's a joke. Grinning down at me . . . His throat was dry. He looked at his watch; why the hell didn't they come? Since they had to, why? *One day I was flying down one of them heavenly streets.* You got yourself into it, Todd thought. Like Jonah in the whale.

"Justa throwin' feathers in eve'body's face. An' ole Saint Peter called me in. Said, 'Jefferson, tell me two things, what you doin' flying' without a harness; an' how come you flyin' so fast?' So I tole him I was flyin' without a harness 'cause it got in my way, but I couldn'ta been flyin' so fast, 'cause I wasn't usin' but one wing. Saint Peter said, 'You wasn't flyin' with but *one* wing?' 'Yessuh,' I says, scared-like. So he says, 'Well, since you got sucha extra fine pair of wings you can leave off yo harness awhile. But from now on none of that there one-wing flyin', 'cause you gittin' up too damn much speed!' "

And with one mouth full of bad teeth you're making too damned much talk, thought Todd. Why don't I send him after the boy? His body ached from the hard ground, and seeking to shift his position he twisted his ankle and hated himself for crying out.

"It gittin' worse?"

"I . . . I twisted it," he groaned.

"Try not to think about it, son. That's what I do."

He bit his lip, fighting pain with counter-pain as the voice resumed its rhythmical droning. Jefferson seemed caught in his own creation.

". . . After all that trouble I just floated roun' heaven in slow motion. But I forgot like colored folks will do and got to flyin' with one wing agin. This time I was restin' my ole broken arm and got to flyin' fast enough to shame the devil. I was comin' so fast, Lawd, I got myself called befo ole Saint

Peter agin. He said, 'Jeff, didn't I warn you 'bout that speedin'?' 'Yessuh,' I says, 'but it was an accident.' He looked at me sad-like and shook his head and I knowed I was gone. He said, 'Jeff, you and that speedin' is a danger to the heavenly community. If I was to let you keep on flyin', heaven wouldn't be nothin' but uproar. Jeff, you got to go!' Son, I argued and pleaded with that old white man, but it didn't do a bit of good. They rushed me straight to them pearly gates and gimme a parachute and a map of the state of Alabama . . ."

Todd heard him laughing so that he could hardly speak, making a screen between them upon which his humiliation glowed like fire.

"Maybe you'd better stop a while," he said, his voice unreal.

"Ain't much more," Jefferson laughed. "When they gimme the parachute ole Saint Peter ask me if I wanted to say a few words before I went. I felt so bad I couldn't hardly look at him, specially with all them white angels standin' around. Then somebody laughed and made me mad. So I tole him, 'Well, you done took my wings. And you puttin' me out. You got charge of things so's I can't do nothin' about it. But you got to admit just this: While I was up here I was the flyin'est son-of-a-bitch what ever hit heaven!' "

At the burst of laughter Todd felt such an intense humiliation that only great violence would wash it away. The laughter which shook the old man like a boiling purge set up vibrations of guilt within him which not even the intricate machinery of the plane would have been adequate to transform and he heard himself screaming, "Why do you laugh at me this way?"

He hated himself at that moment, but he had lost control. He saw Jefferson's mouth fall open. "What—?"

"Answer me!"

His blood pounded as though it would surely burst his temples, and he tried to reach the old man and fell, screaming, "Can I help it because they won't let us actually fly? Maybe we are a bunch of buzzards feeding on a dead horse, but we can hope to be eagles, can't we? *Can't we?*"

He fell back, exhausted, his ankle pounding. The saliva was like straw in his mouth. If he had the strength he would strangle this old man. This grinning gray-headed clown who made him feel as he felt when watched by the white officers at the field. And yet this old man had neither power, prestige, rank, nor technique. Nothing that could rid him of this terrible feeling. He watched him, seeing his face struggle to express a turmoil of feeling.

"What you mean, son? What you talking 'bout . . . ?"

"Go away. Go tell your tales to the white folks."

"But I didn't mean nothing like that . . . I . . . I wasn't tryin' to hurt your feelings . . ."

"Please. Get the hell away from me!"

"But I didn't, son. I didn't mean all them things a-tall."

Todd shook as with a chill, searching Jefferson's face for a trace of the mockery he had seen there. But now the face was somber and tired and old. He was confused. He could not be sure that there had ever been laughter there, that Jefferson had ever really laughed in his whole life. He saw Jefferson reach out to touch him and shrank away, wondering if anything except the pain, now causing his vision to waver, was real. Perhaps he had imagined it all.

"Don't let it get you down, son," the voice said pensively.

He heard Jefferson sigh wearily, as though he felt more than he could say. His anger ebbed, leaving only the pain.

"I'm sorry," he mumbled.

"You just wore out with pain, was all . . ."

He saw him through a blur, smiling. And for a second he felt the embarrassed silence of understanding flutter between them.

"What was you doin' flyin' over this section, son? Wasn't you scared they might shoot you for a crow?"

Todd tensed. Was he being laughed at again? But before he could decide, the pain shook him and a part of him was lying calmly behind the screen of pain that had fallen between them, recalling the first time he had ever seen a plane. It was as though an endless series of hangars had been shaken ajar in the airbase of his memory and from each, like a young wasp emerging from its cell, arose the memory of a plane.

The first time I ever saw a plane I was very small and planes were new in the world. I was four and a half and the only plane that I had ever seen was a model suspended from the ceiling of the automobile exhibit at the state fair. But I did not know that it was only a model. I did not know how large a real plane was, nor how expensive. To me it was a fascinating toy, complete in itself, which my mother said could only be owned by rich little white boys. I stood rigid with admiration, my head straining backward as I watched the gray little plane describing arcs above the gleaming tops of the automobiles. And I vowed that, rich or poor, some day I would own such a toy. My mother had to drag me out of the exhibit, and not even the merry-go-round, the Ferris wheel, or the racing horses could hold my attention for the rest of the fair. I was too busy imitating the tiny drone of the plane with my lips, and imitating with my hands the motion, swift and circling, that it made in flight.

After that I no longer used the pieces of lumber that lay about our backyard to construct wagons and autos . . . now it was used for airplanes. I built biplanes, using pieces of board for wings, a small box for the fuselage, another piece of wood for the rudder. The trip to the fair had brought something new into my small world. I asked my mother repeatedly when the fair would come back again. I'd lie in the grass and watch the sky and each flighting bird became a soaring plane. I would have been good a year just to have seen a plane again. I became a nuisance to everyone with my questions about airplanes. But planes were new to the old folks, too, and there was little that they could tell me. Only my uncle knew some of the answers. And better still, he could carve propellers from pieces of wood that would whirl rapidly in the wind, wobbling noisily upon oiled nails.

I wanted a plane more than I'd wanted anything; more than I wanted the red wagon with rubber tires, more than the train that ran on a track with its train of cars. I asked my mother over and over again:

"Mama?"

"What do you want, boy?" she'd say.

"Mama, will you get mad if I ask you?" I'd say.

"What do you want now, I ain't got time to be answering a lot of fool questions. What you want?"

"Mama, when you gonna get me one . . . ?" I'd ask.

"Get you one what?" she'd say.

"You know, Mama; what I been asking you . . ."

"Boy," she'd say, "if you don't want a spanking you better come on 'n tell me what you talking about so I can get on with my work."

"Aw, Mama, you know . . ."

"What I just tell you?" she'd say.

"I mean when you gonna buy me a airplane."

"AIRPLANE! Boy, is you crazy? How many times I have to tell you to stop that foolishness. I done told you them things cost too much. I bet I'm gon wham the living daylight out of you if you don't quit worrying me 'bout them things!"

But this did not stop me, and a few days later I'd try all over again.

Then one day a strange thing happened. It was spring and for some reason I had been hot and irritable all morning. It was a beautiful spring. I could feel it as I played barefoot in the backyard. Blossoms hung from the thorny black locust trees like clusters of fragrant white grapes. Butterflies flickered in the sunlight above the short new dew-wet grass. I had gone in the house for bread and butter and coming out I heard a steady unfamiliar drone. It was unlike anything I had ever heard before. I tried to place the sound. It was no use. It was a sensation like that I had when searching for my father's watch, heard ticking unseen in a room. It made me feel as though I had forgotten to perform some task that my mother had ordered . . . then I located it, overhead. In the sky, flying quite low and about a hundred yards off, was a plane! It came so slowly that it seemed barely to move. My mouth hung wide; my bread and butter fell into the dirt. I wanted to jump up and down and cheer. And when the idea struck I trembled with excitement: Some little white boy's plane's done flew away and all I got to do is stretch out my hands and it'll be mine! It was a little plane like that at the fair, flying no higher than the eaves of our roof. Seeing it come steadily forward I felt the world grow warm with promise. I opened the screen and climbed over it and clung there, waiting. I would catch the plane as it came over and swing down fast and run into the house before anyone could see me. Then no one could come to claim the plane. It droned nearer. Then when it hung like a silver cross in the blue directly above me I stretched out my hand and grabbed. It was like sticking my finger through a soap bubble. The plane flew on, as though I had simply blown my breath after it. I grabbed again, frantically, trying to catch the tail. My fingers clutched the air and disappointment surged tight and hard in my throat. Giving one last desperate grasp, I strained forward. My fingers ripped from the screen. I was falling. The ground burst hard against me. I drummed the earth with my heels and when my breath returned, I lay there bawling.

My mother rushed through the door.

"What's the matter, chile! What on earth is wrong with you?"

"It's gone! It's gone!"

"What gone?"

"The airplane . . ."

"Airplane?"

"Yessum, jus like the one at the fair . . . I . . . I tried to stop it an' it kep right on going . . ."

"When, boy?"

"Just now," I cried through my tears.

"Where it go, boy, what way?"

"Yonder, there . . ."

She scanned the sky, her arms akimbo and her checkered apron flapping in the wind, as I pointed to the fading plane. Finally she looked down at me, slowly shaking her head.

"It's gone! It's gone!" I cried.

"Boy, is you a fool?" she said. "Don't you see that there's a real airplane 'stead of one of them toy ones?"

"Real . . . ?" I forgot to cry. "Real?"

"Yass, real. Don't you know that thing you reaching for is bigger'n a auto? You here trying to reach for it and I bet it's flying 'bout two hundred miles higher'n this roof." She was disgusted with me. "You come on in this house before somebody else sees what a fool you done turned out to be. You must think these here li'l ole arms of your'n is mighty long . . ."

I was carried into the house and undressed for bed and the doctor was called. I cried bitterly; as much from the disappointment of finding the plane so far beyond my reach as from the pain.

When the doctor came I heard my mother telling him about the plane and asking if anything was wrong with my mind. He explained that I had had a fever for several hours. But I was kept in bed for a week and I constantly saw the plane in my sleep, flying just beyond my fingertips, sailing so slowly that it seemed barely to move. And each time I'd reach out to grab it I'd miss and through each dream I'd hear my grandma warning:

"Young man, young man
Yo arm's too short
To box with God. . . ."

"Hey, son!"

At first he did not know where he was and looked at the old man pointing, with blurred eyes.

"Ain't that one of you all's airplanes coming after you?"

As his vision cleared he saw a small black shape above a distant field, soaring through waves of heat. But he could not be sure and with the pain he feared that somehow a horrible recurring fantasy of being split in twain by the whirling blades of a propeller had come true.

"You think he sees us?" he heard.

"See? I hope so."

"He's coming like a bat outa hell!"

Straining, he heard the faint sound of a motor and hoped it would soon be over.

"How you feeling?"

"Like a nightmare," he said.

"Hey, he's done curved back the other way!"

"Maybe he saw us," he said. "Maybe he's gone to send out the ambulance and ground crew." And, he thought with despair, maybe he didn't even see us.

"Where did you send the boy?"

"Down to Mister Graves," Jefferson said. "Man what owns this land."

"Do you think he phoned?"

Jefferson looked at him quickly.

"Aw sho. Dabney Graves is got a bad name on accounta them killings, but he'll call though . . ."

"What killings?"

"Them five fellers . . . ain't you heard?" he asked with surprise.

"No."

"Eve'body knows 'bout Dabney Graves, especially the colored. He done killed enough of us."

Todd had the sensation of being caught in a white neighborhood after dark.

"What did they do?" he asked.

"Thought they was men," Jefferson said. "An' some he owed money, like he do me . . ."

"But why do you stay here?"

"You black, son."

"I know, but . . ."

"You have to come by the white folks, too."

He turned away from Jefferson's eyes, at once consoled and accused. And I'll have to come by them soon, he thought with despair. Closing his eyes, he heard Jefferson's voice as the sun burned blood-red upon his lids.

"I got nowhere to go," Jefferson said, "an' they'd come after me if I did. But Dabney Graves is a funny fellow. He's all the time making jokes. He can be mean as hell, then he's liable to turn right around and back the colored against the white folks. I seen him do it. But me, I hates him for that more'n anything else. 'Cause just as soon as he gits tired helping a man he don't care what happens to him. He just leaves him stone-cold. And then the other white folks is double hard on anybody he done helped. For him it's just a joke. He don't give a hilla beans for nobody—but hisself . . ."

Todd listened to the thread of detachment in the old man's voice. It was as though he held his words at arm's length before him to avoid their destructive meaning.

"He'd just as soon do you a favor and then turn right around and have you strung up. Me, I stays outa his way 'cause down here that's what you gotta do."

If my ankle would only ease for a while, he thought. The

closer I spin toward the earth the blacker I become, flashed through his mind. Sweat ran into his eyes and he was sure that he would never see the plane if his head continued whirling. He tried to see Jefferson, what it was that Jefferson held in his hand. It was a little black man, another Jefferson! A little black Jefferson that shook with fits of belly laughter while the other Jefferson looked on with detachment. Then Jefferson looked up from the thing in his hand and turned to speak but Todd was far away, searching the sky for a plane in a hot dry land on a day and age he had long forgotten. He was going mysteriously with his mother through empty streets where black faces peered from behind drawn shades and someone was rapping at a window and he was looking back to see a hand and a frightened face frantically beckoning from a cracked door and his mother was looking down the empty perspective of the street and shaking her head and hurrying him along and at first it was only a flash he saw and a motor was droning as through the sun's glare he saw it gleaming silver as it circled and he was seeing a burst like a puff of white smoke and hearing his mother yell, "Come along, boy, I got no time for them fool airplanes, I got no time," and he saw it a second time, the plane flying high, and the burst appeared suddenly and fell slowly, billowing out and sparkling like fireworks and he was watching and being hurried along as the air filled with a flurry of white pinwheeling cards that caught in the wind and scattered over the rooftops and into the gutters and a woman was running and snatching a card and reading it and screaming and he darted into the shower, grabbing as in winter he grabbed for snowflakes and bounding away at his mother's, "Come on here, boy! Come on, I say!" And he was watching as she took the card away seeing her face grow puzzled and turning taut as her voice quavered, "Niggers Stay from the Polls," and died to a moan of terror as he saw the eyeless sockets of a white hood staring at him from the card and above he saw the plane spiraling gracefully, agleam in the sun like a fiery sword. And seeing it soar he was caught, transfixed between a terrible horror and a horrible fascination.

The sun was not so high now, and Jefferson was calling, and gradually he saw three figures moving across the curving roll of the field.

"Look like some doctors, all dressed in white," said Jefferson.

They're coming at last, Todd thought. And he felt such a release of tension within him that he thought he would faint. But no sooner did he close his eyes than he was seized and he was struggling with three white men who were forcing his arms into some kind of coat. It was too much for him, his arms were pinned to his sides and as the pain blazed in his eyes, he realized that it was a straitjacket. What filthy joke was this?

"That oughta hold him, Mister Graves," he heard.

His total energies seemed focused in his eyes as he searched for their faces. That was Graves, the other two wore hospital uniforms. He was poised between two poles of fear and hate as he heard the one called Graves saying,

"He looks kinda purty in that there suit, boys. I'm glad you dropped by."

"This boy ain't crazy, Mister Graves," one of the others said. "He needs a doctor, not us. Don't see how you led us way out here anyway. It might be a joke to you, but your cousin Rudolph liable to kill somebody. White folks or niggers don't make no difference . . ."

Todd saw the man turn red with anger. Graves looked down upon him, chuckling.

"This nigguh belongs in a straitjacket, too, boys. I knowed that the minnit Jeff's kid said something 'bout a nigguh flyer. You all know you caint let the nigguh git up that high without his going crazy. The nigguh brain ain't built right for high altitudes . . ."

Todd watched the drawling red face, feeling that all the unnamed horror and obscenities that he had ever imagined stood materialized before him.

"Let's git outa here," one of the attendants said.

Todd saw the other reach toward him, realizing for the first time that he lay upon a stretcher as he yelled:

"Don't put your hands on me!"

They drew back, surprised.

"What's that you say, nigguh?" asked Graves.

He did not answer and thought that Graves' foot was aimed at his head. It landed in his chest and he could hardly breathe. He coughed helplessly, seeing Graves' lips stretch taut over his yellow teeth, and tried to shift his head. It was as though a half-dead fly was dragging slowly across his face, and a bomb seemed to burst within him. Blasts of hot, hysterical laughter tore from his chest, causing his eyes to pop, and he felt that the veins in his neck would surely burst. And then a part of him stood behind it all, watching the surprise in Graves' red face and his own hysteria. He thought he would never stop, he would laugh himself to death. It rang in his ears like Jefferson's laughter and he looked for him, centering his eye desperately upon his face, as though somehow he had become his sole salvation in an insane world of outrage and humiliation. It brought a certain relief. He was suddenly aware that although his body was still contorted, it was an echo that no longer rang in his ears. He heard Jefferson's voice with gratitude.

"Mister Graves, the army done tole him not to leave his airplane."

"Nigguh, army or no, you gittin' off my land! That airplane can stay 'cause it was paid for by taxpayers' money. But you gittin' off. An' dead or alive, it don't make no difference to me."

Todd was beyond it now, lost in a world of anguish.

"Jeff," Graves said. "You and Teddy come and grab holt. I want you to take this here black eagle over to that nigguh airfield and leave him."

Jefferson and the boy approached him silently. He looked away, realizing and doubting at once that only they could release him from his overpowering sense of isolation.

They bent for the stretcher. One of the attendants moved toward Teddy.

"Think you can manage it, boy?"

"I think I can, suh," Teddy said.

"Well, you better go behind then, and let yo pa go ahead so's to keep that leg elevated."

He saw the white men walking ahead as Jefferson and the boy carried him along in silence. Then they were pausing, and he felt a hand wiping his face, then he was moving again. And it was as though he had been lifted out of his isolation, back into the world of men. A new current of communication flowed between the man and boy and himself. They moved him gently. Far away he heard a mockingbird liquidly calling. He raised his eyes, seeing a buzzard poised unmoving in space. For a moment the whole after-noon seemed suspended, and he waited for the horror to seize him again. Then like a song within his head he heard the boy's soft humming and saw the dark bird glide into the sun and glow like a bird of flaming gold.

Back in the thirties when I was a music student in the South , I was moved to great agonies of empathy by three novels. One of thes was Wuthering Heights, another was Jude the Obscure and the other was Crime and Punishment. While I was reading these works I felt such a compelling identification with their respective heroes that I literally suffered through every trial and exhalted in their every triumph. Evidently I missed many of the subtlties of the thematic structures of these works and I was aware of this at the time, but I missed none of the action and there are memory traces still in my throat which were put there by the poignant and tragic developments of these fictions. Now, I had no idea of ever writing in those days, certainly I had no idea of writing fiction, musical composition was my major interest, . Nevertheless I was moved to a great admiration of the art by these books. And the fact that they could so takeme out of myself and transport me to a more intense world of feeling and acting, yes , and thinking intrigued me more than I realized at the time.

Oddly enough, these works which so moved me did not me to the extent of trying to write. It took a poem, Eliot's Waste Land , to do this. For here was something as intriguing as a trumpet improvization by Louis Armstrong in which rather than the interpolations from classics and popular musical motives Eliot drew motives, lines, etc from earlier poets and thus produces something as intriguing as those two hundred chourses on the theme of ChinaTown for which Armstrong was famous during that period. I dont mean to imply that I thought Eliot's method was the same as Armstrong's , though both are masters of the culture of their respective crafts. Indeed, both know all that has gone before them and both have influenced

ALSO BY RALPH ELLISON

"[One] of the most formidable figures in American intellectual life."
—*Washington Post Book World*

GOING TO THE TERRITORY

The seventeen essays collected in this volume prove that Ralph Ellison was not only one of America's most dazzlingly innovative novelists but perhaps also our most perceptive and iconoclastic commentator on matters of literature, culture, and race. In *Going to the Territory,* Ellison provides us with dramatically fresh readings of William Faulkner and Richard Wright, along with new perspectives on the music of Duke Ellington and the art of Romare Bearden. Erudite, humane, and resounding with humor and common sense, the result is essential Ellison.

Nonfiction/Literature/0-679-76001-6

INVISIBLE MAN

First published in 1952 and immediately hailed as a masterpiece, *Invisible Man* is one of those rare novels that have changed the shape of American literature. For not only does Ralph Ellison's nightmare journey across the racial divide tell unparalleled truths about the nature of bigotry and its effects on the minds of both victims and perpetrators, it gives us an entirely new model of what a novel can be.

Fiction/Literature/0-679-73276-4

SHADOW AND ACT

With intellectual incisiveness and stylish, supple prose, Ralph Ellison examines his antecedents and in so doing illuminates the literature, music, and culture of both black and white America. His range is virtuosic, encompassing Mark Twain and Richard Wright, Mahalia Jackson and Charlie Parker, *The Birth of a Nation* and the Dantesque landscape of Harlem. Throughout, he gives us what amounts to an episodic autobiography that traces his formation as a writer as well as the genesis of *Invisible Man.*

Nonfiction/Literature/0-679-76000-8